PURRFECT SLUG

THE MYSTERIES OF MAX 53

NIC SAINT

PURRFECT SLUG

The Mysteries of Max 53

Copyright © 2022 by Nic Saint

All rights reserved. No part of this book may be reproduced in any form by any electronic or mechanical means including photocopying, recording, or information storage and retrieval without permission in writing from the author.

This is a work of fiction. Names, characters, places, brands, media, and incidents are either the product of the author's imagination or are used fictitiously. The author acknowledges the trademarked status and trademark owners of various products referenced in this work of fiction, which have been used without permission. The publication/use of these trademarks is not authorized, associated with, or sponsored by the trademark owners.

Edited by Chereese Graves

www.nicsaint.com

Give feedback on the book at: info@nicsaint.com

facebook.com/nicsaintauthor
@nicsaintauthor

First Edition

Printed in the U.S.A

PURRFECT SLUG

A Regular Slugfest

When a slug and snail infestation overtook our backyard, it was all our humans could do to get rid of the slimy creatures. And that was even before billionaire Edward Dexter entered our lives. Ed's daughter had gone missing, and so he turned to Odelia to find her. Only that's not how the rest of the family saw it. They thought Odelia was having an affair with the handsome billionaire, and so the trouble began.

In the meantime Harriet was trying to train neighboring dogs Fifi and Rufus for their upcoming dog show. They both wanted to become Best in Show, and Harriet promised she could take them all the way to the top. Too late did she remember the old saying 'Never work with children or animals.' Suffice it to say things didn't go smoothly.

CHAPTER 1

As it happens, a dark cloud had descended upon my hometown. And to think that the day had started out so sunny and bright. But then of course I'm not a fortune teller, so it's always hard for me to know what is going to take place in the near or distant future. All I know is that I woke up experiencing a certain malaise, which is not my custom. And then of course Grace, our human's little girl, discovered that cats have tails, and decided that pulling those tails provides a limitless source of joy, and so she'd been chasing my tail for the best part of the morning. Each time I thought I was safe, and had shaken off the infernal infant, there she was, giggling and gibbering, as human infants are in the habit of doing, and making a dive for my tail, giving it a forceful yank the moment she managed to take hold of the sensitive appendage. Not a pleasant way to pass the morning!

"Why does she keep doing this!" Dooley cried, since he, too, had become a victim of Grace's latest game. So much so that we'd taken cover in the backyard, hiding behind the rose bushes, where Grace had yet to root us out.

"She seems to derive a certain pleasure from the process,"

I said as I nervously scanned the horizon, just in case our newfound nemesis staged a comeback.

"But why? What's so funny about pulling a cat's tail?"

"I'm not sure," I said, "but it seems there is something inherently fascinating about a tail that appeals to the youthful zeal these infants possess in spades."

It was one more aspect of cohabiting with a human infant that we hadn't taken into account on that fateful day when Odelia had announced that soon two would become three, and that our home was to be blessed with Kingsley offspring.

So far I hadn't experienced much of the joy a baby is supposed to bring. If Grace wasn't pulling our tails, she was vomiting all over our precious fur, or digging a chubby little hand into our food bowls and spreading kibble across the kitchen floor, like a farmer sowing seeds. Or dunking certain objects into our drinking bowls, such as there are: a rubber ball, a pacifier, or a stuffed elephant.

"Oh, where are the days when it was just us and Odelia," I said with a deep sigh, as I placed my head on my front paws, without relaxing my vigilance, lest our formidable foe suddenly appeared out of the blue, as she often does.

"It's all Chase's fault," said Dooley. "If Odelia hadn't met him, she wouldn't have married him, and if she hadn't married him, Grace wouldn't have shown up."

And as we both moodily stared before ourselves, silently blaming Chase Kingsley for this horrible predicament we found ourselves in, a tiny voice suddenly sounded in my ears. It wasn't Grace, that much was obvious, for she might be a baby, but she has a voice like an opera singer when she's going well.

No, this voice was so weak it could have been my tummy rumbling and expressing its distress at having to drink water laced with stuffed elephant residue, or eating kibble that has been used to sweep the kitchen floor.

"Help me!" the tiny voice called out.

I glanced over to my friend. But Dooley's lips weren't moving, and unless he'd suddenly turned into a ventriloquist, it was clear it wasn't him asking for help.

"Can you please help me!" the voice repeated, a little louder this time, and more emphatically.

So I glanced around in all directions, my head turning this way and that, and that's when I finally saw it: a snail was sneaking along the branches of the rose bush we were currently using as cover. The snail was staring at me with helpless bewilderment, and repeated, "Help me, please! I'm hanging on for dear life here!"

As far as I could tell, the snail was firmly glued to that branch, as snails do, and wasn't in any immediate danger. Still, obviously she or he—or it—was going through a personal crisis of some kind, for its feelers waved back and forth, as if trying to draw my attention, and then it said, "It-it's going to eat me!"

"What's going to eat you?" I asked, curious about this creature's distress.

"What's going to eat what?" asked Dooley, who'd opened his eyes to take in the strange scene. "Oh, hey there, little guy. How are you doing?"

"Not well, cat," said the snail. "If I'm not careful, that big bird is going to eat me with hide and hair!"

"I didn't know snails had hair," said Dooley, interested. "Though I can understand how being eaten is not a fun prospect. I wouldn't like it myself."

"Please chase it away," said the snail. "I know birds don't like cats, and so if you could please do me this one little favor, I'll make it worth your while."

I looked around for a sign of this bird the snail was talking about, and lo and behold: there was indeed a bird, perched on the top branch of the rose bush, eyeing our slimy little friend with distinct relish reflected in its beady eyes.

"Now shoo, bird," I said sternly, and waved an admonishing paw in the direction of the bird. "Take a hike, will you? Nothing to see here so move along."

The bird shifted its gaze from the snail to me, and didn't seem to like what it saw, for it frowned darkly. "If you know what's good for you, you won't come between me and my meal, cat," said the bird with a sort of menacing undertone.

"And what if I do?" I said, not liking the attitude of this bird one little bit.

I'd raised myself up to my full height, which, I have to say, is considerable, and to my satisfaction I saw how the bird seemed to flinch a bit when it saw what it was up against. So finally the bird—it could have been a sparrow, or it could have been a robin, my knowledge of the different bird species is shamefully limited— growled, "Oh, all right. Have it your way." And after directing one final longing look at our new friend the snail, it spread its wings and flew off, to live and catch another snail another day, I guess.

"Phew, tanks, cat," said the snail, as it visibly relaxed now that the danger had passed. "That bird had been following me around for quite a while now!"

"I don't understand why birds eat snails anyway," said Dooley. "Isn't it difficult to digest, with all of that slime? And not very tasty either, I would imagine."

"And let's not forget about the shell," I said. I couldn't imagine trying to swallow down a whole shell. I'm sure it would feel like a brick in my stomach. Then again, birds are strange creatures. And probably possess concrete stomachs.

I'd already taken my position underneath that bush again, preparatory to taking a light nap, when the snail said, "I said I'd make it worth your while, and my name wouldn't be Rupert if I didn't keep my promise. So here goes, cats."

"Here goes what?" asked Dooley, glancing around to see what other slimy creatures would come crawling out from the undergrowth.

"It's an expression, Dooley," I said as I stifled a yawn. "It means he's going to do something."

"Do what?"

"I don't know. Something." Frankly I was feeling a little sleepy right around then. I guess it was because of the adrenaline dissipating from my system. That and being chased around the house by Grace had sapped my strength. So whatever wisdom the snail was intent on imparting, I scarcely paid attention, and even as I dozed off, I was conscious of strange words being spoken by the snail.

"Blue moon," he said. Or words to that effect.

If only I'd paid closer attention, and hadn't allowed my natural vigilance to waver at that crucial moment, it might have saved me a whole lot of trouble!

CHAPTER 2

Tex had been pottering around in his backyard, weeding the flowerbeds and thinking up ways and means of beautifying his modest little patch of paradise, when his thoughts of floral delight were rudely interrupted by his neighbor Ted, who desired speech.

"Say, Tex," said Ted, his head popping up over the hedge that served as a natural barrier between both gardens. "I've been thinking."

"Well, that's a first," Tex muttered under his breath, as he reluctantly downed tools. It wasn't that he disliked his neighbor, but it couldn't be said he liked him a great deal either. There had always existed a certain rivalry between both men, especially when it came to the fate of their respective backyards. Tex had long been a big proponent of the common garden gnome as a way of lending that little *je-ne-sais-quoi* to his property, and Ted had more or less brazenly copied the idea. The result was a sort of garden gnome race between the two homeowners.

"I've been thinking we should pool our resources and hire

a professional landscaper," said Ted, as he rubbed his nose then sneezed.

Tex frowned at his neighbor. "What are you talking about? What landscaper?"

He'd gotten up from his position on the foam pad he used to protect his knees and approached the hedge. At one point they'd agreed to a fence to mark the official boundary, but recently had decided that a hedge was much nicer, and also provided a way for their respective pets to come and go as they pleased. Ted and his wife Marcie owned a sheepdog, Rufus, who, contrary to popular belief, wasn't an enemy to the Poole cat contingent but a friend, and so as Ted and Tex chatted across the hedge, Tex saw that Harriet and Brutus scooted underneath, and crossed into Ted's backyard to shoot the breeze with the man's canine friend.

"Look, I know you take great pride in your backyard, Tex," said Ted. "And you know I do, too. But at the end of the day, we're hardly pros, are we? And you have to admit it takes a lot of time and effort to make these gardens shine. So I was thinking that maybe if we bring in a landscaper, and then pay a gardener to come in once a week, or once every two weeks, we could save ourselves a lot of trouble, and at the same time have the kind of backyards we can really be proud of."

"Mh," said Tex as he gave this suggestion some thought. The idea had merit. Though he was reluctant to admit it to his neighbor, of course. So instead he said, "Professional landscapers are expensive, Ted. Even if we pooled our resources."

"Oh, I'm sure between the two of us, it's a warranted expenditure," said Ted. With a wink, he added, "I might even be able to turn it into a tax deduction."

Ted was an accountant, so creating tax breaks or write-offs was what he did.

"I'd have to discuss it with Marge," said Tex, wavering. He enjoyed working in his backyard, but lately he'd started feeling the strain, especially when spring was in the land, of spending every available moment having to fight the good fight against the pesky weeds attacking his flowerbeds. Even the modest patch of lettuce and radish he'd planted at Marge's instigation needed constant vigilance to save them from a veritable army of pests trying to get at them before Tex could.

"Look, I know you need some time to think about it," said Ted, "but give it some serious thought, yeah? I think you'll find it will make both our lives a lot easier. And hey, paying a gardener doesn't mean we can't still do a little bit of gardening ourselves. Only difference is that we'll have fun doing it, and not see it as a chore we can't get out of." He shrugged. "At least that's how I feel. You?"

Tex slowly nodded. "Lately it's all becoming a little too much," he admitted. "Especially those snails that keep eating everything I plant."

"Yeah, same here," said Ted. "And you should see what they're doing to my gnomes. Every morning those little buddies are full of slimy trails. Really yucky."

It was a problem the good doctor had been contending with himself, and he could sympathize.

"I just hope this landscaper of yours goes easy on the toxic products."

"Oh, no! Natural stuff only," Ted assured him. "Absolutely. We don't want to poison the soil, now do we?" And with a final nod at his neighbor, Ted returned to the arduous work of having to clean his gnomes from all traces of snail slime.

It was an arduous task, and a thankless one at that. For no sooner had they cleaned their respective gnomes, an army of snails had defaced them again.

And so it was with a faint sense of hope that Tex returned

to his weeding. For once in his life, Ted had had a good idea. An idea Tex could wholeheartedly get behind. And if this gardener proved a tax break, so much the better. Your hardworking doctor has to count the pennies, just like any responsible family man.

CHAPTER 3

While Tex stood chatting with his neighbor, Harriet and Brutus had slipped through the hedge and were now engaged in earnest conversation with Rufus, the Trappers' sheepdog. As a rule, cats and dogs don't usually see eye to eye, but then life in Hampton Cove doesn't always adhere to the fixed rules that seem to govern the rest of the world.

"I don't think so, Rufus," Harriet was saying. "I really believe you should go through with it."

"But Harriet," Rufus said, directing a look of anguish at his neighbor. "How can you be so sure?"

"Because you are just about the handsomest dog I know, that's why," said Harriet. A rare compliment in her book, but one that was well deserved, she felt.

"I don't know," said the big fluffy dog, as he hung his head, prey to indecision. "What if I lose badly? I'll never live it down. You know what pets are like."

Oh, she most certainly did. Once she had given her all by launching herself into show business, only to be laughed off the stage by a roomful of haters. So she could see where

Rufus was coming from. Which is why she felt so adamant about this. "Look, Rufus," she said, deciding to go for broke. "If you do this, I'll be there for you every step of the way. And I'm talking personal one-on-one coaching. I'll be your personal trainer, mental coach and psychologist all rolled into one."

"And me," said Brutus, a little gruffly, Harriet felt. "Don't forget about me."

"You would do that for me?" asked Rufus, a smile breaking through the clouds.

"Of course!" said Harriet. "And if you make it, which I'm sure you will, it will be because we gave it everything we had. It will be a celebration of the art of perseverance." And her personal vengeance against all the naysayers that claimed she was a talentless hack. Of which, she had to say, there were plenty.

"What about you, Brutus?" asked Rufus, consulting Harriet's mate. "Do you think I should sign myself up for this dog show or not?"

Brutus hesitated for a moment, but then caught Harriet's eye. "Of course," said the butch black cat. "I think you're a very talented dog, Rufus, and it's about time the world saw you for who you are."

Rufus beamed widely. If even Brutus felt that their friend had a chance, he might as well go ahead. "Could you give Fifi the same speech you just gave me?"

"Fifi?" asked Harriet. "Does she also want to join the show?"

"Oh, absolutely," said Rufus. "In fact it was her idea. Only she doesn't feel she's pretty enough to enter such an important competition, so she bailed."

"I think Fifi stands just as much chance as you," said Harriet, and hoped her words rang true with the power of conviction. She'd never understood why dogs enter these

Best in Show deals, but then she'd always relied more on her innate sense of talent rather than her good looks. But it was certainly true that both Rufus and Fifi were prime specimens of their respective species, and would have no trouble finding plenty of supporters to defend their claim at the big prize.

"Okay, if I've got you both in my corner, I think I might give this thing a shot," finally Rufus decided. He heaved a deep sigh. "Now all we need to do is to convince Ted and Marcie to enter me into the competition. And Kurt, of course."

They exchanged worried glances. Convincing Ted and Marcie was one thing, but Fifi's human was quite another. A retired schoolteacher, the notoriously bad-tempered Kurt Mayfield wasn't the kind of person to take advice from his neighbors, and the only way to enter both dogs in the competition was for Harriet to tell Gran or Marge, and for Gran or Marge to talk to their neighbors and float the idea. If either Rufus or Fifi's humans decided against the idea, no dice!

"Oh, it will be fine," said Harriet, as she gently patted the big dog on in the flank. "Kurt will have to agree. He just has to."

"If Fifi doesn't sign up, neither will I," said Rufus, in a strong example of canine loyalty.

"Fifi will sign up. And if Kurt refuses," said Harriet, "we'll sign her up in secret. He'll never even know she entered the show until it's all over and done with."

"Yeah, but someone has to walk her onto the platform," said Rufus. "And if not Kurt, then who?"

Harriet smiled a fine smile. "Just leave that to me," she said, as an idea was already starting to form in her resourceful mind.

CHAPTER 4

The snail incident was soon forgotten, especially when it transpired that once again Grace had gotten it into her nut to freely distribute our food supply across the kitchen floor. Only this time it wasn't kibble but the contents of a pouch of wet food, and so when Odelia found her daughter sitting on the floor of the kitchen, hands and face liberally smeared with premium cat food, and also her clothes and part of the floor and even the walls, she heaved an exasperated groan, and picked up her daughter to remove the remnants of our lunch from the girl's person.

"Now what are we supposed to eat?" I grumbled as I sat beside my empty bowl.

"The fact that Grace likes our food is a good sign," said Dooley. "Babies have an innate sense of taste and smell. They instinctively know what's good for them."

"I think you'll find that's actually cats, Dooley, not babies. A baby will put anything in its mouth, whether it's good for them or not. Which is why most parents confine their infants to a playpen when they're old enough to crawl, so they can't go around putting all kinds of stuff into their mouths, including our lunch!"

Honestly I was waiting for the day that Grace would become a regular upstanding human, just like the rest of them, and stopped messing around and making a nuisance of herself. But as Odelia had explained, this would take a number of years. Humans, as we all know, are very slow, and take many years to turn into adults. And then of course there are those humans who never fully grow up, and remain infants all of their lives. If Gran is to be believed, this includes all the males of the species, though I'm not sure if she was speaking in jest or not.

Chase came wandering into the kitchen, took one look at our empty bowls and our pleading pitiful expressions, and emitted a low chuckle. "Always hungry, aren't you, fellas?" And then he shook his head and walked out again.

"He seems to believe it was us who emptied our bowls," Dooley lamented.

"Yeah, dads will always defend their young," I said. "So even though Grace is the culprit here, as far as her dad is concerned, she's as innocent as a newborn baby."

And since no more food was forthcoming, we decided to skedaddle. If there's one thing we're good at, it's admitting defeat when it's staring us right in the face.

And so we left the kitchen through the pet flap and ventured out into the backyard once more. Where we almost bumped into Harriet and Brutus, who had selected that moment to venture into the house.

"Don't bother," I said. "Grace smeared all of our food across herself and the kitchen floor, and Chase seems to think we ate it all, so it's another day of dieting."

"I'm not interested in food, thank you very much," said Harriet, as if the mere thought of tucking into a full plate of food disgusted her. "In actual fact we're here to argue Fifi and Rufus's case."

"What case?" I asked, not following our friend's reasoning.

"Well, Rufus wants to compete in the upcoming dog show, and so does Fifi, only they both need to secure permission slips from their humans. So now we want Odelia or Marge or Gran to talk to Ted and Marcie and Kurt about it."

"Good luck with that," I said. "Kurt Mayfield will never allow Fifi to enter any competition. He's dead set against that kind of malarkey, as he calls it."

"I know, which is why I was thinking that Odelia could take Fifi. I mean, who's to know Fifi isn't hers? The jury won't know, and it would make Fifi so happy."

It certainly was a good idea, and I saw no flaws in her reasoning. Except one.

"What if Kurt finds out? He'll be furious. And you know how Odelia hates upsetting her neighbor."

"There's no way Kurt will find out. Unless Fifi wins, of course, and her name and picture are printed in the paper. But we all know she doesn't stand a chance."

"Doesn't stand a chance of what?" asked a familiar voice in our rear. When we slowly turned, we saw that we'd been joined by the lady of the hour: Fifi herself.

"Oh, nothing," said Harriet quickly.

"For your information, when I enter a competition, I intend to win," said Fifi, proving that she'd heard the entire conversation. And from the way she sat there frowning at us, it was obvious she didn't like the implication of Harriet's words.

"I didn't mean it like that, Fifi," said Harriet quickly. "What I meant was—"

"Oh, I know perfectly well what you meant, Harriet," said

Fifi coldly. "And even though I appreciate you trying to help me, I'll tell you right now that I don't need any help." She eyed us one by one, fixing us with a frosty look. "From any of you!"

And with these words, the otherwise mild-mannered Yorkie turned on her heel and strode off, back to the hole in the fence that she'd dug there herself, to provide easy coming and going.

Harriet eyed me uncertainly. "Do you think I should go after her and apologize?"

"Better let her cool off a little first," I said. "Obviously she didn't like it when you said there's no chance in hell she'll ever win this competition."

"That's not what I said and you know it!"

"No, but it's what you meant, and it's certainly what Fifi understood."

Harriet looked thoughtful. "She said she doesn't need our help. But how can she possibly enter the competition if Kurt doesn't sign her up? Or Odelia?"

"I don't know," I said. Then again, we all know Fifi as a resourceful canine. If she wanted to enter the competition, there was no doubt in my mind she would.

CHAPTER 5

Odelia had just given Grace a bath when her phone chimed its cheerful tune.

"Can you pick that up, Chase!" she bellowed. "My hands are wet!"

Chase, who'd been busy in their home gym—a euphemism for the spare bedroom where he'd stored some of his fitness equipment—came hurrying up and grabbed his wife's phone. Checking the display, he said, "It's your boss. Should I pick up or let it go to answerphone?"

Odelia didn't hesitate. "Pick up. Maybe it's important."

Dan only phoned when it was urgent. Otherwise he respected her privacy too much to bother her on a day off.

"Hello, Dan," Chase boomed into the phone with his sonorous voice. He listened for a moment, then clapped eyes on Odelia before replying, "How important is this assignment, Dan? On a scale of one to ten, for instance."

"Oh, let me have it," said Odelia, who'd dried her hands. "Yes, Dan? What's this about an important assignment?"

"Do you remember when billionaire businessman Edward Dexter came to town?" asked the senior editor.

"Sure. I interviewed him for the paper."

"Yes, you did. And asked him some very pertinent questions, if I remember correctly. Questions he didn't like very much."

"Yeah, he wasn't happy with me," she said, remembering the incident well. She'd still managed to earn the man's respect, in spite of her harsh line of questioning, or perhaps because of it. No doubt very few reporters had ever grilled him to such an extent. "So what about him?"

"He's in town, and he wants to talk to you."

"Me? But why?"

"No idea. All I know is that he called me out of the blue, and asked if I could arrange an interview with my star reporter as soon as possible."

"Well, sure," she said. "Did he say what he wanted to talk to me about?"

"Nope. Tight-lipped as ever. Just that he wants to meet you at your earliest convenience."

She glanced down at Grace, who was giving her a gummy smile. "I could see him tomorrow, I guess."

"He wants to see you in one hour, in the bar of the Star Hotel. And he said to come alone."

Odelia cast a quick look at her husband, who was floating a rubber duck in front of Grace and getting himself pretty soaked in the process. "I guess that would work. Though I wonder what he wants from me."

"If we're lucky, another exclusive interview," said Dan, and she could almost hear him salivating at the prospect. "How are you fixed for a babysitter?"

"I've got the best babysitter in the world right here," she said, and received a grin from Chase in return.

Once she'd hung up, she told her husband about the interview.

"Are you sure you don't want me to come?" asked Chase

with a touch of concern. "You know what these billionaires are like. They think they own everything and everyone. And if I remember correctly, this guy took quite a shine to you last time you met."

"I'll be fine," she assured him. "We're meeting in a public place, so if he tries anything funny, I'll kick him in the shin and then I'll scream the place down."

"Okay, but whatever he says, don't go up to his room."

"Of course not," said Odelia, smiling at his concern. "I might take Max and Dooley, though."

"Didn't he say to come alone?"

"Yeah, but I don't think he was talking about my cats."

"Brats!" said Grace as she reached for the rubber duck, which her dad had held out of reach while he was talking to Odelia.

"Mommy is going out," Chase explained as he handed Grace the treasured yellow object, which she immediately put into her mouth and started gnawing on with non-existent teeth. "Yes, she's a high-powered reporter, your mommy is. And a very important billionaire wants to talk to her about his billionaire business."

Odelia checked her face in the mirror. She looked terrible. If she was to meet Ed Dexter in less than an hour, and look presentable, she had to get a move on!

CHAPTER 6

Odelia had an assignment for us, and even though justly I could have refused, considering how cavalier she was being with our food supply, I decided not to let the liberties her daughter took with the contents of our bowls put the kibosh on a working relationship that went back years, and had always proved mutually beneficial.

So while Harriet and Brutus got busy prepping Rufus for his big show, and Fifi was off flying solo, Dooley and I hopped into our human's aged pickup for her meeting with the billionaire who'd summoned her on such short notice, dragging her away from her maternal duties.

"He must be a very important person, for you to abandon Grace like that," said Dooley as we took our positions on the backseat, digging in our claws while the car accelerated and was soon hurtling along the route.

"I'm not abandoning Grace," said Odelia. "But it's true that Ed Dexter is a very important person. He's the guy who puts batteries in cars and satellites in space."

"Oh, so he builds cars, does he?" I asked.

"His main business is building batteries, but when he saw

an opportunity, he started building cars, too, figuring they were a good bet for his battery business. And since then he's gone from strength to strength."

"I wonder what he wants to see you about."

"Maybe he wants to sell you a new car," Dooley suggested. "Could be that he saw you in this old wreck and decided you could use a better one."

Odelia smiled at us in her rearview mirror. "I wouldn't mind a new car."

Frankly she could use the replacement, since her own car is falling to pieces. And with a kid to take care of, she'd already expressed a fervent wish to trade her rusty pickup in for a family vehicle. A minivan, perhaps, or a Volvo. Though Chase was still resisting the transition, hoping she would change her mind, and buy a sporty model instead. A Porsche, maybe. Or a fancy Lexus. Knowing Odelia, though, that minivan is going to happen, whether Chase likes it or not.

"Why is it that men hate minivans so much, Max?" asked Dooley.

"I think they feel it emasculates them," I said.

"What is emasticate, Max?"

"Emasculate," I said, enunciating clearly. "It means that a man feels threatened in his masculinity."

"Men of a certain age fight hard against the notion that they're aging fast," Odelia explained. "Especially when they become dads. It really brings home to them the fact that they're getting older. And one of the things they use to hang onto their youth is a sports car, since a lot of boys dream of one day owning one. So now they can finally afford to buy their dream car, only they also have a family to consider, and babies and sports cars don't go well together."

"I think minivans are great," I said.

"Yes, I don't feel dismasticated one bit," said Dooley.

"Emasculated," I said, "with the E of Eek!"

"Let's hope Edward Dexter invited me over to give me an electric minivan," said Odelia. "Though somehow I doubt it."

I did, too. Most billionaires aren't big on giving away stuff for free. Otherwise they wouldn't be billionaires in the first place.

She soon directed her car into the underground parking garage that caters to the Star Hotel's clientele, and once she'd made sure her pickup was locked—though I could have told her there was no need, since no one in their right mind would steal the old thing—we headed to the elevator, and soon arrived in the lobby of the hotel, just in time for our rendezvous with the elusive Mr. Dexter.

We found the businessman in the bar, as arranged, and when he saw that Odelia hadn't come alone, as requested, but had brought along her feline posse, a cloud passed across the man's face. But then he seemed to mentally take the hurdle, and welcomed Odelia by spreading his arms and opening the sluice gates of charm that made him such a fixture in financial circles and social media alike.

"Miss Poole," he said warmly. "Though Dan tells me it's Mrs. Kingsley now?"

"It is," said Odelia, as she took the proffered seat and settled in across the table from the man.

Edward Dexter was a distinguished man in his early fifties, with an unruly mop of dirty blond hair, a patrician nose that slashed the air with decision, straight thin lips, and steely blue eyes that seemed to cut right through you.

He was also thin, which gave me the impression that he probably ran marathons when he wasn't counting his billions or putting batteries in his battery-operated cars or flying off into space in one of his spaceships.

He was impeccably dressed in a pink shirt with blue stripe, and a tie with little bitcoin signs. All in all a man to be reckoned and definitely not trifled with.

"So what can I do for you, Mr. Dexter?" asked Odelia.

The man smiled. "Straight to the point. I like that. Yes, Odelia—may I call you Odelia?—there's something on my mind only you can help me with, I'm afraid."

"Oh?" she said, returning his steely glance with the noncommittal look of the reporter who's burning with curiosity but determined not to show it.

"I don't think he's going to offer her a car, Max," said Dooley.

"No, somehow I have the impression he's in some kind of trouble," I said, studying the man closely, just in case his intentions turned out to be less honorable than expected.

Suddenly the man's spine seemed to collapse, and his shoulders slumped. A sad look came over him, and he said, almost in a whisper, "I've lost the one person most dear to me, Mrs. Kingsley. And frankly I don't know what to do."

"What do you mean?" asked Odelia.

"My daughter," said Mr. Dexter. He glanced left and right, then lowered his voice even more. "I'm afraid she's been taken. She might even be dead already."

CHAPTER 7

"When I was a young man," Mr. Dexter explained, "still trying to find my place in the world, I was fueled by this powerful desire to be successful. A burning desire to make something of myself. You see, my family didn't have a lot of money, and as a kid I often had to witness my mother cry when she had trouble making ends meet. So I vowed one day to become so rich that I could buy her a big house, and set her up with all the amenities she needed, making sure she was happy and didn't have to worry about money ever again. And it was this desire that fueled me all these years, and led me to where I am today."

"One of the wealthiest men in the country," said Odelia, who was probably thinking this was newspaper gold. Then again, I wasn't sure the billionaire was pouring his heart out for the purposes of an article.

"The only problem was that I was so busy setting up one business after the other, and trying to find a way to hit the big time, that I neglected my personal life, to such an extent that I didn't even bother to look for a partner. And so when I finally managed to make my first million, I found myself alone, with no one to share my success with, apart from my parents, who were understandably proud, but also worried that I would end up alone."

"But at least you were able to fulfill your dream," said Odelia.

He nodded, and when a server came, he ordered drinks for both himself and Odelia. The moment the man was out of earshot, he resumed his tale. "When I was thirty, I finally met someone through a mutual friend, and within a year we were married and pregnant with our daughter. Only disaster struck and my wife was taken from me. Luckily the doctors managed to save the child, and ever since that day Addie has been the most important person in my life. We've always been close, to the point that I see her taking over from me at the head of the company one day. She is that smart, that driven, and as dedicated as me."

"But you said she's gone missing?"

"Yes, about two months ago Addie went on a coast-to-coast road trip with her boyfriend Ted. Ted Machosko. I wasn't too worried, as she's a responsible person, and so is Ted. And besides, these days it's so easy to stay in touch, through your phone or Skype or whatever."

"So what happened?"

"Well, for the first part of the trip she reported back to me almost daily. I'd told her the only way I was going to allow her to go was if she took along a state-of-the-art satellite phone, hooked up to one of my satellites, just in case she passed through an area with bad cell phone reception. And I also told her to call me every day. And for a couple of weeks everything seemed to be going really well. She was happy, posting little videos of their trip, and regular updates on her social media. But then all of a sudden two weeks ago the updates stopped, and she also stopped calling. So obviously I got worried, but when I tried calling, there was no connection. As if she'd disappeared from the face of the earth."

"Did you try to pinpoint her location through her phone?"

"Yes, of course. Only both of her phones had stopped transmitting a signal. Either she'd turned them off or..." A look of despair filled his eyes. "Or they were destroyed. I contacted the local authorities of the last place where she was seen, and one man, a gas station owner, remembered seeing her and Ted pull up with their RV and fill up their tank. But that's the last time anyone saw them. Addie, Ted, the RV—gone. Not a trace of them." The server returned with their drinks— coffee for the battery tycoon and tea for Odelia, and once the man was gone, he continued, "It's been two weeks, and frankly I'm at the end of my rope, Mrs. Kingsley."

"Odelia, please."

He smiled weakly. "Which is when I remembered our interview, and Dan telling me you have a knack for solving unsolvable crimes in this town."

"Dan is too kind," Odelia muttered modestly.

"I want you to know that I've practically abandoned any hope of ever seeing my daughter alive again."

"You think something happened to her?"

"I do. This isn't like Addie. She would never just disappear on me like that. Either she was abducted or... worse."

Odelia nodded as she toyed with her teabag. "Where was she last seen?"

"Well, that's just it," said Mr. Dexter. "You'd think she would have disappeared in the desert, or some godforsaken place in the middle of nowhere. But the last person to see her alive said he saw them head in the direction of town."

Odelia frowned. "What town?"

"Well, your town. Hampton Cove."

CHAPTER 8

"How can anyone disappear in Hampton Cove?" asked Dooley. "This town is so small, it's impossible to disappear, even if you wanted to."

Odelia was still engaged in a discussion with Edward Dexter, jotting down a few more details about his daughter and her boyfriend, but Dooley and I were one step ahead: we were already thinking how we could be instrumental in finding this lost daughter.

"I guess a person could disappear anywhere," I said. "Especially if that person didn't want to be found." We exchanged a meaningful look.

"You think Addie Dexter and her dad fell out and now she doesn't want him to find her?"

"It's certainly a possibility," I said. "Maybe their relationship wasn't as harmonious as Mr. Dexter is leading us to believe, and Addie felt the only way to sever the relationship with her parent was to disappear. You have to understand that a man like Dexter has a lot of resources at his disposal to track down his daughter, so she would have to come up with a plan if she didn't want to be found."

"But they seem to get along so well, father and daughter. And he's even training her to be his successor."

"Well, maybe that's the whole point, Dooley. Maybe Addie doesn't want to be his successor, but he's forcing her to follow in his footsteps."

"Maybe she wants to be a juggler instead," said Dooley.

I eyed him with a touch of skepticism. "Why a juggler?"

"Why not? Maybe she joined a traveling circus and is now living the dream as an anonymous juggler named Jackie. Jackie the Juggler."

"And what about her boyfriend? Is he a juggler, too?"

"No, he's probably a clown." He sighed and gave me a fervent sort of look. "I'll bet they're very happy together, Max. Living in their circus caravan, surrounded by a warm and loving community of other circus artists, just like them."

"Mh," I said, though I had to admit it was certainly something we needed to look into. It wouldn't be that hard to find out if a circus had traveled through town. Perhaps they were still in town, and Addie was performing her juggling tricks in plain sight for the whole world to see. Though she would have to disguise herself, of course.

"If she has joined the circus, I think we should respect her choice and not tell her dad," said Dooley, getting ahead of himself a little. "I think we owe it to this young couple's future happiness. And Mr. Dexter will simply have to find himself a different person to succeed him at the head of his multi-billion-dollar corporation."

"Yes, well, there's also the other possibility," I pointed out.

"What possibility?"

"That foul play is involved."

He gaped at me. "You mean..."

"That Addie Dexter has come to harm, and is now wounded or... dead."

He clasped a paw to his furry face, a look of distinct shock in his eyes. "Oh, no!"

"Oh, yes. When a person is missing for so long, and no ransom demand has been made, it's possible that something happened to her and she's dead. Could be that Addie and Ted were in the wrong place at the wrong time, bumped into some bad people, and were murdered, the murderers having disposed of the bodies."

"Oh, Max, we have to find her body! We owe it to her grieving father to bury his daughter!"

And gone was the notion that Mr. Dexter was in fact the bad guy, driving his one and only daughter to face an uncertain future as a traveling juggler. At any rate, it was a mystery we certainly could be instrumental in solving. Cats are part of a large community, and so if Addie Dexter had passed through town, chances were that one of our kind had seen her, and so it behooved us to find out what had happened to the missing girl.

"One last thing, Odelia," said Mr. Dexter. The meeting was coming to a close, and the billionaire and Odelia had risen to their feet and Dooley and I to our paws. "This is very important. Could you conduct your investigation in absolute discretion, please?"

"Of course."

"For now, don't write about Addie's disappearance in your paper. You'll notice that I haven't launched a public appeal. I haven't gone on television or to the papers, and for good reason. Once people find out about what happened, this town will be overrun with fortune seekers. The fact that Addie is my daughter will bring out the worst in people. And trust me, I've seen it happen before, and it's the last thing I want."

"You mean people will try to cash in on a possible reward?"

"Oh, absolutely. It's going to be a gold rush, and before you know it, hundreds or perhaps thousands will flock to Hampton Cove, destroying potential clues and hampering your investigation."

"I'll be discreet," Odelia promised. "I will only confide in people I absolutely trust, and won't tell anyone anything they don't need to know."

"Thank you so much," said Mr. Dexter, and I could tell that he was touched, as he held onto Odelia's hands and shook them warmly.

"Oh, look, Max. It's Gran," said Dooley.

And indeed: through the window that offered an excellent view of the outside dining area, Gran was staring intently in our direction, her face practically plastered to the glass, and looking none too pleased for some reason.

"She'll be able to help Odelia find Addie Dexter," said Dooley. "Gran knows everyone in town, and people trust her."

"Mh," I said. Gran's face spelled storm, her lips moving wordlessly as she stared daggers in our direction. Whatever was bothering her, it seemed big.

But then Odelia and Mr. Dexter said their goodbyes for now, and Odelia even gave the stricken billionaire a warm hug, and so I soon forgot all about Gran's strange behavior. We had a clear mission: find Addie Dexter and bring her home to her dad. And by golly I was going to do my darndest to make it happen.

We passed out of the bar and soon were going down to the parking garage in that same elevator.

"Well?" asked Odelia. "What do you think?"

"I think she's a juggler," said Dooley, firmly sticking to his theory. "But Max thinks she was murdered."

"I don't think she was murdered," I protested. "All I said was that either she disappeared voluntarily, or else she came to some kind of harm, in which case we need to find out what happened."

"I'm not sure I'm the right person for the job," Odelia confessed. "I didn't tell Mr. Dexter, of course, but if the police can't find this girl, what chance do I have?"

"In other words: Mr. Dexter gave you a mission impossible," I said.

"More or less," she said thoughtfully.

"Did he promise you a new car if you find his daughter?" asked Dooley.

"No, he did not," said Odelia with a laugh. "Though there is a reward."

"Reward money? How much?" asked Dooley.

"Fifty thousand. The man is desperate, I could tell."

"Poor man," said Dooley. "He probably won't be happy to know that his daughter wants to be a juggler, but he still needs to be told."

"Let's not jump to conclusions," Odelia suggested as we climbed back into her car. "Let's take this one step at a time, and approach the problem methodically."

"In other words, you want us to start talking to potential witnesses," I said.

"Yes, please, Max," said Odelia. "And in the meantime I'll go and have a little chat with my uncle."

"You think your uncle kidnapped Addie?" Dooley asked.

"No, Dooley, but as the chief of police he will know about Addie Dexter's disappearance, and possible leads that have been pursued." She shrugged as she started the car. "No sense in going over the same territory twice."

CHAPTER 9

Vesta Muffin had been savoring a cup of hot chocolate with plenty of cream on top and some colorful sprinkles. It was a daily ritual she enjoyed with her best friend Scarlett Canyon. Both women were seated in the outside dining area of the Star Hotel, when she happened to see her granddaughter Odelia in earnest conversation with that billionaire guy. That Edward Dexter. He of the cars and the satellites and the rocket ships.

"Hey, isn't that Odelia?" said Scarlett, who had noticed the same thing.

"Mh," said Vesta, not well pleased. "I wonder what she's up to."

"Probably interviewing the guy for the paper," Scarlett suggested, as she took a sip from her frappuccino, then took a nibble from her chocolate chip cookie.

"I hope so. I wouldn't like to be the one having to tell her husband that his wife was caught cheating on him with a billionaire."

"Oh, dear," said Scarlett. "And they just had a baby, too."

"It happens," said Vesta with a sigh of disapproval. "It's a hormonal thing, or so I've been told. So soon after giving birth a woman's body is a raging cauldron of hormones, and it's at times like these, when they're so very vulnerable, that these billionaire playboys will strike."

She narrowed her eyes at the couple, and saw to her surprise that Odelia seemed to be leaning in, as if to comfort the billionaire, who was holding his head in his hands, clearly in the grip of some powerful emotion.

Her expression hardened. "Not on my watch," she growled. She was a firm believer in live and let live, and for a person to chart their own course through life, but not when the well-being of her great-granddaughter was at stake.

"Such a pity," said Scarlett, gently tut-tutting even as she studied the big chunk of cherry cream cake she'd placed on her fork, preparatory to unloading its rich flavor onto her tongue and let her taste buds have at it. "And here I thought they were such a devoted couple, Odelia and Chase."

"That's what I thought," Vesta said as she weighed her options. She'd already taken out her phone and was snapping a couple of shots of the lovebirds, and shot a short video for good measure. She hadn't yet formulated a plan of campaign, but at least she'd have visual evidence of Odelia's affair with the billionaire.

"On the other hand, it must be nice to have a billionaire in the family," Scarlett said. "I mean, I like Chase, don't get me wrong, but a cop's salary doesn't exactly stretch very far, when you get right down to it. And I've always wanted one of those electric cars."

Vesta shot her friend a not-so-friendly look.

"What? What did I say?"

"I don't believe this," said Vesta, shaking her head.

"It doesn't have to be a big one. A small one will do."

"So you'd throw over Chase, just on the off chance that this Dexter fella would get you an electric car."

"Well, electric cars happen to be the future, and unfortunately they're too expensive for my budget." She shrugged. "A girl can dream, can't she?"

"Dream on," Vesta growled. "Odelia is breaking up with Chase over my dead body." And to show her friend she wasn't kidding, she promptly got up and headed over to the window, which offered an excellent view of the bar, where the frolicking couple were enjoying those first happy moments of a new courtship. And as she snapped a couple more pictures, she suddenly noticed that Max and Dooley were seated right next to her granddaughter's chair!

"Well, I'll be damned," she grunted.

"What is it?" Scarlett asked, and since she hadn't noticed her friend joining her at the window, she jumped a foot in the air, and almost dropped her phone.

"What are you thinking, sneaking up on me like that!" she cried.

"He is handsome, isn't he? And a widower, if Wikipedia is to be believed."

"Look, there's no way I'm allowing my granddaughter to hook up with this guy, so just get those sordid thoughts out of your head right now."

"Oh, all right," said Scarlett. "Don't get your knickers in a twist."

"I'm putting an end to this right now," she said, and got busy typing a strongly worded message, adding the video and the pictures she shot as evidence. "There," she said. "Now let's see her ignoring her duties as a wife and mother now."

Not to mention a pet parent. What was she thinking, dragging those impressionable cats along to her date with a billionaire? Didn't she know that setting a bad example like that could scar those precious little dears for life?

"If this family didn't have me," she said, taking her position at the table again, "God knows what kind of trouble they'd get into."

CHAPTER 10

Marge Poole was assisting her husband in the backyard, weeding and removing dead leaves and heads from their precious flowers. She was outfitted for the occasion with rubber gardening gloves, her straw gardening hat and her gardening boots, and as the sun shone down on her back, she felt intensely satisfied when she regarded her work: the flowerbed that had been infested by weeds and bugs and whatnot once again looked vividly colorful and full of life—the kind of life your amateur gardener likes to see: absolutely devoid of pests.

"So what do you think, honey?" asked her husband, who was manicuring his herbaceous border until it looked fit for duty.

"About what?" she asked, taking a firmer grip on her little trowel.

"Well, Ted's idea about the landscaper."

"Oh, I don't know," she said. "Is it really worth the expense? I mean, we only have a very modest little garden, so I don't think a landscaper will have enough to work with, let alone a gardener."

"But we could join forces, us and the Trappers: get rid of that hedge and join our two backyards into one big one."

"I'm not sure that's such a good idea," she said as she dug her trowel into the earth. "That hedge is there for a reason. It's so we can have some privacy, and so can the Trappers. Otherwise what's the point of having your own backyard? We could just as well cut down all the hedges and all the fences in the entire neighborhood and create a park."

"Now why didn't I think of that?" said Tex. "We should create one big park where all the kids could play! And then I could organize a barbecue for the entire neighborhood! Now wouldn't that be fun?"

She gave her husband a skeptical look, which passed right over his head. "Let's give it some more thought, shall we?" she suggested. Most of her husband's more harebrained ideas rarely survived a couple of days' serious reflection. Once Tex saw how impractical his idea was, he forgot all about it. Besides, she liked to do some sunbathing in her backyard from time to time, and if they cut down that hedge, that would be a thing of the past. No woman likes to sunbathe with the Ted Trappers of this world breathing down their neck.

Her phone buzzed, alerting her that a message had arrived, and she took it out of the front pocket of her gardening coveralls. When she saw the first line of the message, she frowned. 'Evidence of YOUR daughter's CHEATING WAYS!!!!!!'

"Now what?" she murmured. At the same time, her husband's phone also dinged, and for a moment they both studied the message Ma had sent. Then they turned to face each other, their mouths agape.

"I don't believe this," said Tex.

"Neither do I," Marge agreed.

But there it was, clear as day: video and pictures of their

one and only daughter, her arms around famous billionaire Edward Dexter, clearly having an intimate moment!

Just then, Grace made a gurgling sound. The little girl had been safely ensconced in her playpen, which Marge had placed on the terrace for the occasion, with a big umbrella to shade the little one from the sun.

"Oh, dear," said Marge as she brought a distraught hand to her face. "What's going to become of Grace now?!"

CHAPTER 11

"Okay, Rufus, it's very important that you do exactly as I say." Harriet gave the sheepdog a hard look, hoping her words would penetrate the big dog's sluggish brain. "There's a certain routine we need to nail down, and when I say nail, I do mean you'll have to nail it if you want to stand a chance at winning that gold cup."

"Gold cup?" said Rufus. "I thought being selected Best in Show came with a year's supply of Dog Snax?"

"Yes, it does, but more importantly, you will take home that very beautiful and very coveted gold cup."

Rufus gave her a look of confusion. "Now what do I want with a gold cup?"

"You can put it on your mantelpiece," said Harriet, trying to hold onto her equanimity. Now she understood why all the dog trainers she'd seen on YouTube all looked old and gray. Dealing with dogs took a lot of patience, which was wearing really thin by now. "It's all about the honor," she said, when Rufus still didn't get it. "You want to make your humans proud, don't you?"

"Well, sure," said Rufus.

"So? That cup will make Ted and Marcie very happy. They'll be able to show it off to their friends and family."

"And that's what makes them happy? Being able to show off a gold cup?"

"Of course. Humans love to show off to other humans. It's one of their favorite pastimes. They buy cars so they can show them off to the neighbors. Clothes to show off to their colleagues. Husbands to show off to their friends. Wives to show off to their golf buddies. That's why they call it a trophy wife. Now let's take it from the top. You have to jump over that hurdle, and make sure you don't trip."

They'd selected one of Ted's hideous gnomes as a stand-in for the first hurdle in the concourse, and if Rufus managed to clear it in one go, he just might stand a chance. So far he hadn't been able to, but they still had plenty of time. The competition was next Saturday, which should be a cinch... for a talented dog.

"Such a pity that Fifi couldn't join us," said Brutus, who was Harriet's co-trainer. "It would have been nice if Rufus and Fifi could have trained together."

"Fifi decided she didn't need our services," said Harriet with a touch of hauteur. "So if she doesn't make it into the competition, it's her own fault."

"I know, but maybe one of us should go over there and try to talk to her again. It might give Rufus a boost. Just look how unhappy the big guy looks."

They both eyed the big sheepdog with a critical eye, and Harriet had to admit her partner was correct: Rufus did look a little lethargic. Even as he approached the big gnome, his heart didn't seem to be in it. And as he jumped, trying to clear the hurdle, once again he managed to topple the thing.

"You have to take a running leap!" Harriet yelled. "How many times do I have to tell you!" Shaking her head, she stalked over to her inept pupil, and proceeded to put the gnome upright again. "Yuck, it's slimy," she said as she quickly removed her paw from the monstrosity.

"It's the snails," said Rufus sadly. "They have been crawling all over the garden, sliming everything. It's driving Ted and Marcie crazy."

"Okay, let's try again," said Harriet, the fate of her neighbors' backyard not of any concern to her. "And this time I want to see some energy! Some vigor!"

"Yes, Harriet," said Rufus with a deep sigh, and slouched off to give it another shot.

No, his heart clearly wasn't in it. And so with the quickness of decision that was typical of her, she decided that Brutus was right, and that Fifi had to be conciliated, whatever the cost.

"Brutus, better go and apologize to Fifi," she said therefore. "And tell her to join us."

"You want me to apologize?" said Brutus.

"Of course. I can't apologize. I'm the trainer. And apologizing to a trainee would undermine my position. Whereas you are merely an assistant trainer, which means your role is to get in good with the trainees. Boost morale."

"If you say so," said Brutus dubiously.

"It's a good cop, bad cop kind of situation," she explained, seeing that her mate hadn't fully grasped the concept. "Now get her over here. And quick, before I lose my patience!"

She watched Brutus toddle off, and shook her head. If she'd known how hard this training thing was going to be, she would never have accepted the position.

And as Rufus scratched his flank with one of his hind legs, trying to work out what he was doing wrong, Harriet's keen ears picked up an interesting conversation taking place one backyard over.

"I can't believe this," Marge was saying. "Odelia cheating on Chase with Edward Dexter? It's impossible."

"And yet here's the photographic evidence," Tex said. "Our daughter, in the arms of that playboy billionaire."

"But why? I thought she and Chase were so happy."

"If there's one thing I know, it's that it's very hard to know what goes on in other people's marriages, honey. Odelia may look happy, but clearly she isn't, otherwise she would never throw herself into the arms of another man like this."

"Poor Chase. And poor Grace. What's going to become of that poor baby?"

"Odelia will get custody, of course. And Chase will get visitation rights. And then Grace will have a billionaire for a daddy. Which maybe isn't such a bad thing."

"How can you say that! I thought you loved Chase like a son?"

"I do love Chase like a son, but what can we do? We'll just have to accept that soon we'll have Edward Dexter as our son-in-law."

"It must be one of those things," said Marge. "A coup de foudre. It happens."

"And clearly it happened to Odelia."

And as the disturbing discussion raged on, suddenly Harriet caught sight of an even more upsetting sight: Marcie Trapper stood listening very carefully to the conversation next door, and from the red flush of her cheeks and the sparkle in her eyes, she was enjoying every single moment, and recording it for posterity—or so she could spread the terrible news to the rest of the neighborhood!

CHAPTER 12

We found Uncle Alec in his office, from where he oversees the law enforcement efforts of his troops. Though when we entered the office, the Chief wasn't overseeing his troops so much as staring out of the window, idly gazing in the direction of Town Hall, where his girlfriend is mayor of our town.

The moment we walked in, he quickly turned, as if caught doing something he shouldn't.

"Oh, it's you," he said, relaxing again.

"Who did you think it was?" said Odelia as she joined him at the window. "And what are you looking at?"

Her uncle heaved a deep sigh, replete with silent sorrow. "It's Charlene."

"Uh-oh. Trouble in paradise?"

He gave his niece a strange look. "Funny you should say that. Charlene wants to go on holiday with me."

"So? Isn't that great?"

"It would be our first holiday together. And you know what they say about a couple's first holiday?"

"That they're fun? Exciting? Practically like a honeymoon?"

"A minefield. And possibly a death knell for the relationship."

Odelia laughed. "What are you talking about?"

"Oh, you know how it is. Now we see each other from time to time. Some evenings we spend at my place, some at her place, and some evenings we spend alone, and I like it like that. Things are going well, so why change things up?"

"Okay, but if Charlene wants to go on holiday with you, what's so bad about that?"

"Everything!" he said, throwing up his arms in a gesture of despair. "We'll spend every single minute of every single day together, and before you know it the inevitable will happen and we'll get into a fight, and then it will be all over!"

"Or you could have a great time together and grow closer as a couple."

"I doubt it," the Chief grumbled, clasping his hands behind his back and scowling at a passing bird that had done him no harm whatsoever. "Once she gets to know me—the real me—she'll get tired soon enough. She'll complain that I snore too much, eat too much, drink too much and that my feet are too cold."

"If your feet were cold she'd know it by now. Same thing about the snoring, or the eating and the drinking. You've been together how long now?"

"A year," the Chief grunted unhappily.

"If she didn't like you, don't you think she would have left already?"

"I dunno," he mumbled.

"Look, the fact that she wants to go on holiday together is a big step, Uncle Alec. It means she's serious about this relationship, and she wants to move forward. Take the next big step."

He looked up, startled. "You mean... move in together?"

Odelia nodded. "Why not? You like her, she likes you, and you have to admit you're good together."

"But I don't want to move in together!"

"Just take this trip," Odelia suggested. "And if everything works out and you end up having a great time, which I know you will, you can think about the next step."

"I don't want there to be a next step," he grumbled. "I like this step."

Odelia smiled, and patted her uncle on the back. "It's going to be all right," she assured him. "Just you wait and see."

He gave her a funny look. "Look, I know you're a big girl, Odelia, but don't you think that what you're doing right now..." He hesitated, then tried again. "I mean, you know I like Chase, don't you? In fact I love the guy like the son I never had."

"Of course I know that," said Odelia. "And I'm sure he does, too."

"So..." But the Chief shook his head, then grunted, "It's none of my business."

Odelia frowned, but didn't pursue the matter. It was obvious her uncle was working through some personal issues, and needed time to figure things out.

"So what do you want, anyway?" he asked, returning to his desk, where a large portrait of Charlene stood facing us. He took it in one of his big hands, studied it for a moment, sighed deeply, and put it in one of his drawers, shoving it shut.

"I've been asked by Edward Dexter to find out what happened to his daughter," said Odelia, not wasting time getting to the point.

Uncle Alec's brow furrowed at the mention of the billionaire's name. "Dexter," he growled, as if the man had personally insulted him. "Does Chase know about this?"

"Oh, absolutely."

"So it's official, is it?"

"Of course. Though I doubt he'll have time to help me find Ed's daughter."

"Mh," said the Chief, staring at his niece with a dubious sort of look on his mug. "Okay, go on. What's this about a missing daughter?"

"Well, Addie Dexter went on a road trip with her boyfriend Ted a couple of weeks ago. The idea was that they would travel from coast to coast in their RV, so they set out from San Francisco and were going to drive all the way up to Montauk, then south to Florida to join Ed, who's got a place down there. Only they never made it past Hampton Cove, and disappeared without a trace two weeks ago. No messages, no phone calls, and her phone was switched off. So Ed is worried."

"Naturally," the Chief grumbled unhappily.

"He told me he reported Addie and Ted missing, so I was wondering about the state of the investigation. He felt fobbed off, so I wanted to check in with you."

"What I would like to know is why this guy," said the Chief, planting two beefy arms on his blotter and fixing his niece with a critical look. "Why Ed Dexter? Is it the money? I mean, I know Chase isn't a billionaire, but money isn't everything, honey. Chase has heart, and that's what matters. And he's got plenty of it."

"I know he does, Uncle Alec," said Odelia. "But he also has a job to do, so I can't ask him to find Addie. And besides, like I said, Edward tells me he already talked to the police, and they couldn't help him."

"He didn't talk to me, that's for sure. If he had, I'd remember."

"I think he talked to Randal. Who told him that Addie

probably decided to go off the grid for a while. Kids do that kind of stuff all the time. He told him not to worry."

"Yeah, that sounds like Randal, all right," said the Chief with a grimace. "So why didn't he bring his case to me? I would have organized a search. Clearly if this girl has gone missing, we need to find her."

"He doesn't want to involve too many people," Odelia explained. "He's afraid that the media will get hold of the story, and then all hell will break loose."

"Yeah, I can see his point," the Chief admitted reluctantly. "If word got out that Edward Dexter's daughter went missing in Hampton Cove, every nut in the country would descend on this town, hoping to collect whatever reward money they can get." He arched an inquisitive eyebrow. "There is a reward, isn't there?"

"There is, but obviously I'm not going to collect it if I find Addie. I told him to donate the money to a charity of his choice. But first I have to find the girl."

"Mh, I'll bet he'll give you some other reward, too," the Chief muttered, earning himself an odd glance from his niece.

"Look, I understand that you don't like Edward," said the latter. "Most people don't. And I admit he's an acquired taste. But once you get to know him, he's a wonderful man. Sensitive, intelligent, and very, very worried about his daughter."

"Of course, of course," said the Chief, holding up his hands in a placating gesture. "So what do you want me to do?"

"Talk to Randal. Ask him what he discovered, if anything. And then tell me."

"Okay, fine," said the Chief, getting up. But before he reached the door, he turned, and gave his niece an earnest look, placing both hands on her shoulders. "I just... I hope you know what you're doing, honey."

"Of course," said Odelia, surprised by the man's heartfelt look and the moistness of his eyes. "And thank you for taking this to heart, Uncle Alec."

"How could I not," said the Chief, choking up.

CHAPTER 13

"Look, Fifi, Harriet didn't mean what she said. Of course you're a great candidate. I bet you can even win this whole thing."

Fifi gave Brutus a look that was devoid of those warm sentiments the little dog usually reserved for her friends and neighbors.

"I heard what I heard, Brutus," she said. "And besides, if Harriet wants to apologize, why doesn't she do it herself? Why send you?"

"I told you already. Because she's so busy training Rufus. Getting him ready for the big show." Brutus would have wiped away a bead of sweat, if he could have without Fifi noticing. This apologizing thing was harder than he thought. And besides, Fifi was right: it should have been Harriet pouring apologetic phrases into the little Yorkie's ear, not him.

"Look, don't you want to train together with Rufus? Work as a team?"

"There's no I in team, Brutus," said Fifi haughtily. "And

since a dog show isn't a team effort, it's every dog for himself from now on. And that goes for Rufus, too!"

"But he's floundering, Fifi! Rufus is suffering. His head isn't in the game, and if only you would join him, I just know he'd be over the moon."

"He should have thought of that before he hired Harriet as his personal trainer."

"But..."

"No means no, Brutus. Rufus and I go our separate ways, and that's my final word."

And then she stalked off in the direction of her own backyard, presumably to continue her training. Brutus watched her leave, and a distinct sense of doom and gloom settled over him. But only for a moment. He was, after all, a cat not particularly prone to experiencing the finer emotions, and so he quickly shrugged off Fifi's refusal. If she wanted to go it alone, so be it. It was her funeral. And if Rufus didn't want to put his back into it, then that was his business.

And as he set paw in the direction of the Trappers' backyard, where most of the action was taking place, he suddenly caught sight of a peculiar creature. If his eyes didn't deceive him, it was one of those creatures that carry their own house on their back. Which had always struck him as very inconvenient. Imagine he would carry an entire house on his back. He'd never get anywhere. Which was probably why these snails, as they were called, moved so infernally slow.

"Pssst!" the snail was saying.

It was located on the leaf of his favorite rose bush, the one he and Harriet liked to single out when they were feeling frisky.

He toddled over, wondering what this snail wanted from him. Maybe to help carry its load?

"Hey, cat!" the snail said, indicating that it really did want speech with him.

So he approached the creature, took a tentative sniff, and said, "What do you want?" He wasn't feeling in a particularly bonhomous mood. He might not care that Fifi was out of the race, but he did care about Harriet's opinion, and he knew that when he returned empty-pawed, so to speak, she would be none too happy.

"I talked to one of your lot this morning," the snail announced, "and after he saved me from that bird, I promised I'd make it worth his while."

"I have absolutely no idea what you're talking about," said Brutus.

"It wasn't you. It was some orange fatty," said the snail.

Brutus grinned. "Yeah, that's Max. He's pretty fat, and pretty orange. But don't tell him I said that. He doesn't like it when you call him—"

"Fat?"

"Orange. So Max saved your life, did he? Typical. He's always saving someone from something."

"Okay, so now I'm confused. Is this Max a friend of yours or what?"

"I guess you could say that," Brutus admitted. He and Max might not always see eye to eye, but he did consider him one of his best pals.

"Could you give him a message from me? I would tell him myself, but I gotta run."

Brutus laughed. A running snail. Now there was something he'd never seen before. But the snail seemed dead serious.

"Just tell him that this blue moon business we talked about this morning is happening tonight. I can smell it."

"That's it?" asked Brutus.

"Yeah, he'll know what I mean," said the snail. "So you'll deliver the message?"

"Of course. Blue moon happening tonight. Got it."

"Thanks, buddy," said the snail, and started moving down the flower's stem, at a snail's pace.

"What's your name, by the way?" asked Brutus, watching the snail's progress with fascination.

"Rupert," said the snail. "You?"

"Brutus."

"Well, see you around, Brutus," said Rupert. "And don't let the bed bugs bite."

"What bed bugs? What are you talking about?"

But Rupert had disappeared into the rose bush's inner workings, and so their discussion was at an end.

Brutus shrugged and went on his way. He hated being the bearer of bad news, especially when the recipient was Harriet. But that couldn't be helped.

Moments later he was lumbering through the hole in the hedge, and when he came face to face with his beloved, and she saw he was alone, she tsk-tsked freely.

"She doesn't want our help!" he cried. "And I couldn't make her, could I?"

"Fifi isn't coming?" asked Rufus in his big, booming voice.

"Nah. She wants to go it alone," said Brutus.

"Oh, that's too bad," said Rufus, and promptly plunked down on the grass and proceeded to stare off into space, looking sad and despondent.

"Now look what you've done!" Harriet whispered. "Our star pupil, and you've taken the wind right out of his sails!"

"I didn't take any wind out of any sails. Fifi did," he argued. But it was no good, of course. They'd lost what could very well have been a shoo-in for the big prize, now a victim to a distinct lack of motivation.

"I should have known," said Harriet, as she threw her star a nasty look. "Never work with children or dogs. Everybody knows that, so why did I think I could make it work?"

And since the training was on hiatus for the moment,

they both wandered back into their own backyard, where Marge and Tex still stood discussing the future of their daughter's marriage.

"Oh, that's right," said Harriet. "I almost forgot to tell you."

"Tell me what?"

"Odelia and Chase are getting a divorce."

He stared at his mate. "What?!"

"Yeah, Odelia is having an affair with a billionaire. Edward Dexter, the guy who makes those exploding cars and shoots celebrities into space? Well, he's her new beau, and so she's kicking Chase to the curb."

Brutus produced a low whistle. "Well, how about that?"

"Yeah, and so she'll probably sell the house and move in with him, cause who wants to live in a dump like this when you can live in a castle?"

"Edward Dexter lives in a castle?"

"He's a billionaire, Brutus. Of course he lives in a castle." A dreamy look came into her eyes. "I'll bet he's got the best cat food in the world. The good stuff, flown in from Fiji."

"What's a Fiji?"

"It's a country, Brutus. Try to keep up, will you?"

"Okay," he said, having a hard time doing just that. "So what's going to happen to Grace?"

"Oh, she'll live with us, of course."

"Us? You mean you and me and Chase?"

Harriet gave him a scathing look. "Of course not. You and me and Odelia and Mr. Billionaire Playboy."

"Okay," he said. But then a thought occurred to him. "So what about Chase? Where is he going to live?"

Technically Chase was still his human, so it probably mattered a great deal where he was going to live, for he might insist that Brutus live with him, away from the others.

"Who cares where Chase lives? He'll probably go crawling back to New York, his tail between his legs."

"Chase has a tail?" he asked. He'd never noticed.

"Oh, Brutus," said Harriet with a look of exasperation. "Sometimes I wonder if I shouldn't find myself a playboy billionaire."

CHAPTER 14

*O*fficer Randal Skip had neglected to do his duty when he told Addie Dexter's dad that he shouldn't worry. That his daughter was probably having a great time off-grid with her boyfriend, and that she'd be home soon. After Uncle Alec had told Officer Skip what he thought of such dereliction of duty, he informed Odelia of same, and so when we were out in the parking lot in front of the police station, Odelia summed things up nicely when she said, "I guess we're exactly nowhere, you guys."

"I think that's exactly true," I riposted.

"At least now we know that Addie is having a great time with her boyfriend off-grid and she'll be home soon," said Dooley, as usual offering an alternative view of things.

"I very much doubt Addie is having a great time," I told my friend. "From what Edward told us, Addie would never leave her father in the dark like this. So unless she and her dad had a falling-out, I think it's safe to assume something bad happened to her. And it's up to us to find out what."

"I hope Chase has some idea of where to start," said

Odelia as she headed in the direction of her car. "Cause I sure don't."

And we'd almost reached the car when a familiar face inserted itself between ourselves and Odelia's pickup.

"So is it true?" asked this person. "Are congratulations in order?"

It was Ida Baumgartner, one of our small town's biggest gossips, and also Tex's most loyal patient, with always some new disease to keep the doctor on his toes.

"Congratulations?" asked Odelia. "Oh, you mean Grace."

"That's right, Grace. What's going to happen to the little one?"

"Why, she'll stay with us, of course," said Odelia, puzzled.

"I thought so," said Ida, nodding knowingly. "I told Rory Suds that Grace would stay with you, and I'm happy to know I was right." She patted Odelia on the arm. "It's always best in these cases, trust me. And I do hope you won't leave us. Hampton Cove could use this shot in the arm. In fact this just might be the best thing to happen to this town in a long time. It's going to put us on the map. Tourism will get a big boost, of course, not to mention the local economy." She beamed upon Odelia like a proud mother goose upon a favorite gosling. "Well done, you. Well done." She placed her hands together in impromptu applause. Then she was off again, leaving us to stare after her, much bewildered.

"What was that all about?" I asked once we were back in the car.

"I have no idea," said Odelia. "Maybe Ida finally lost her last marble?"

"I didn't know Ida still played with marbles," said Dooley.

But at that moment Odelia's phone belted out a tune and she picked up with a cheerful, "Just the person I need! Can you help me find Addie Dexter?"

"Why? Did you lose her?" Chase's voice sounded through the car.

"I didn't, but her dad did."

"So how was it?"

"The poor man is devastated."

"I wouldn't exactly call him poor," said Chase. "I googled the guy, and as of this morning he's worth two hundred billion dollars."

"Not bad for a guy who sells cars," Odelia quipped. "But seriously, his daughter Addie went missing on a road trip, and he asked me to find her."

"Why? I mean, don't get me wrong, I think you're crazy talented, babe. But you're not exactly a professional people finder."

"He doesn't want to attract attention, and he's heard good things about me. Mainly from Dan, but still. And it helps that I know this town like the back of my hand."

"This girl went missing in Hampton Cove?"

"That's right."

"Of course I'll help you. But are you sure you don't want your uncle to organize a search party?"

"Like I said, Edward wants to handle this on the down-low. He's afraid that once word gets out this town will turn into a circus."

"See?" said Dooley. "I knew she'd joined the circus. Her and her boyfriend."

"Okay, so it's just the two of us, huh?"

"I'm afraid so," said Odelia.

"Great. As if I didn't have enough to contend with at the moment."

"Tough day at the office?"

"Something like that. Listen, I'll see you tonight, and then we can talk this thing through and get organized. I'll tell your uncle to give me the rest of the week off and we'll find this girl. How does that sound?"

"Like music to my ears, babe."

"Circus music," said Dooley.

CHAPTER 15

*D*ooley felt adamant that he was on the right track when it came to finding Addie Dexter. She'd probably had a taste of freedom, with this long road trip she'd taken, and didn't want to go back to her old life, which she probably saw as the proverbial golden cage now. And so she'd decided to join a traveling circus.

And a good thing, too!

Why shouldn't a person join the circus? It was a fun life, juggling balls and cones for a living. You met all kinds of interesting people, fraternized with lions and elephants, and you could sleep under the stars—or was that traveling hobos?

At any rate, all he had to do now was to convince Max of his idea, and that's where he'd hit a snag. His friend might have a brilliant mind, but he also had a stubborn streak, and wasn't always open to new ideas when they didn't fit in with his own ideas.

"I still think we should look into this circus thing, Max," he said therefore. "I'm sure that's where we'll find Addie and Ted."

"Odelia asked her uncle, but there hasn't been a circus in

town for months," said Max. "So she couldn't possibly have joined them."

See? Stubborn. "So maybe the circus was in the next town?" he suggested patiently. Sometimes he felt as if he had to do all the thinking for Max, and now was one of those times. "Or maybe two towns over? It could even be three."

"We'll look into it, Dooley," said Max, but he said it in a patronizing sort of way, Dooley felt. As if he didn't really think the idea had merit.

"Or maybe they joined a group of traveling musicians," he now suggested, just to keep the ball rolling. "You know, like a band or something. They could have joined the Traveling Wilburys."

"I think you'll find that the Traveling Wilburys are on hiatus," said Max. "On account of the fact that most of them are dead. And anyway, they never did a lot of traveling, even when they were still a full set."

"I'm just spitballing here," he said, and was starting to feel that all of his best ideas were simply going to waste.

"We'll look into everything you've suggested," said Max. "But first we need to talk to Chase, and see what he comes up with. We'll organize a meeting tonight, put all of our ideas on the table, and take it from there. How does that sound?"

Dooley smiled. Max really was the greatest. "That sounds like a plan," he said, well pleased. Max had listened to him after all, just like he knew he would.

He sighed happily. Quite frankly there wasn't a better friend in all the world than Max.

§⁂

"We have to do something. For the sake of my great-granddaughter," said Vesta. She'd hurried home and was now conferring with her daughter and son-in-law in the kitchen. "You did see the pictures and the video I sent you, didn't you?"

"I did," said Marge, looking and sounding depressed. "You saw this with your own eyes?"

"And so did Scarlett," said Vesta.

Scarlett, who was seated at the kitchen table next to her, nodded solemnly. "They looked very cozy together," she said. "And when the tryst was over they disappeared into the lobby, and according to the receptionist they walked into the elevator together, probably to continue their lovers' meeting upstairs, in the guy's room."

"My God," said Marge, placing a palm to her temple to soothe the throbbing vein there.

"I find this very hard to believe," said Tex. "I mean, this is Odelia we're talking about. She's always been the most sensible one of us all. And the sanest one." He directed a meaningful look at Vesta, which the latter decided to ignore.

"It's a coup de foudre," she said. "Scarlet called it, didn't you, hun?"

"It can happen to the best of us," said Scarlett. "It happened to me many, many times. Like when I met your husband, Vesta."

"Fine, all right," Vesta was quick to say. "Let's not go there."

"No, I guess we better don't," Scarlett murmured as she hastily cast down her eyes.

"We have to talk to her," said Marge. "And I think it's best if I do it, as her mother."

"Or we could organize an intervention," Tex suggested. "Sit her down and point out her responsibilities as a mother and a wife."

Grace, who must have sensed that all eyes had turned to her, now gurgled a happy refrain. "Gloo gloo!" she yammered, pumping the air with a pudgy fist.

"Poor kid," said Scarlett. "Good thing she's too young to realize what's going on."

Vesta's son Alec entered the kitchen, looking slightly harried, the few remaining strands of hair on his head in disarray. "I'm sorry I'm late," he said, panting a little as he pulled up a chair. "Charlene had us visiting a travel agent."

"Oh, that's right. You're going vacationing together," said Scarlett. "Have you picked a destination yet?"

"No, we have not," said Alec emphatically. "And I'm not sure we ever will."

"Oh, but why? Going on holiday as a couple is one of the best things about being married."

"We are NOT married," said Alec, from between gritted teeth.

Obviously Scarlett had hit a nerve, and wisely chose to back off.

"We're thinking about staging an intervention," Marge said, filling the newcomer in on the plans. "Sit her down and try and talk some sense into her."

"How sure are we that Odelia and this Dexter fella are an item?" asked Alec.

"Always the cop," said Vesta, throwing up her hands. "Always looking for evidence." She tapped her phone, which she'd placed on the table. "Aren't the pictures I sent you evidence enough? Or the video?"

"All I see is Odelia hugging some dude," said Alec. "Doesn't mean they're having an affair. Heck, if I had an affair with every woman I hug, I'd be exhausted."

He looked exhausted, Vesta thought. His cheeks, otherwise so plump and rosy, were pale, his skin wrinkly and saggy.

"Are you coming down with something?" she asked, placing a hand on her son's forehead. But of course he slapped her hand away.

"I'm fine," he grunted irritably. "Have you sent these pictures to Chase already?"

"Of course not."

"And why not, if I may ask? He has a right to know that his wife is cheating on him."

"We don't want to cause any trouble," said Marge, "before we have a chance to confront Odelia. There may be an innocent explanation."

"Innocent explanation, my ass," said Vesta. "You should have seen them. As lovey-dovey a couple as I've ever witnessed. No, those two are in love. And I should know. I'm an expert at this stuff."

Ever since her own husband had cheated on her with Scarlett, she'd had a firm distaste for cheaters. Even when those cheaters were her beloved granddaughter. Still, Marge was right. They had to give Odelia a chance to explain. And to change her evil ways.

"I say we confront her, and tell her to dump this billionaire," she suggested.

"She'll come to her senses, I'm sure," said Marge, always the optimist. "And Chase never needs to know." She looked around the table searchingly. "Are we all in agreement? If Odelia agrees to stop seeing her billionaire, we don't tell Chase?"

"All those in favor, raise your hand," said Vesta. Much to her satisfaction, she saw they had a full quorum.

"Let's save a marriage, people," she concluded. "And save a little girl's future."

"Broom broom!" Grace bellowed, always wanting to have the last word.

CHAPTER 16

*D*ooley was looking at me intently, and so I said, "We still haven't considered Dooley's idea about the circus."

Odelia and Chase were seated in their salon, with Dooley and myself also present. Maps had been researched, and possibilities for a search examined and quickly discarded, since Addie's dad didn't want his daughter's disappearance to become widely known just yet.

Odelia frowned. "The circus? What are you talking about, Max?"

"I think she might have joined a traveling circus," Dooley piped up. "To escape her dad, who may not be as kind and sweet as we think."

Odelia thought about this for a moment, then nodded.

"What are they saying?" asked Chase.

"That Addie might not have been kidnapped but might have joined a traveling circus instead, to get away from her dad."

Chase gave me an appreciative look. "Excellent thinking," he said.

"It wasn't my idea," I hastened to say. But of course he didn't understand me.

"It's entirely possible that Addie and her dad didn't get on as well as he says they did," said the cop as he frowned at a map of Hampton Cove which lay spread out on the coffee table. "So where did Dexter say she was last seen?"

"Right here," said Odelia, pointing to a spot on the map.

"And she told someone they were headed in this direction?"

"Yes, the owner of the gas station where they filled up the RV. They said they'd traveled all across the States, and were going to keep traveling east until they reached Montauk, and then go south, all the way to Florida, where they would take a well-deserved break before returning home."

"Okay, so to reach Montauk they had to pass through Hampton Cove," Chase mused as he traced the possible route the couple had taken with his finger. "And that was also the last time their cell phone signal was picked up?"

"Yes, Addie's phone had a tracker app, so her dad could always see where she was. And the last time her phone transmitted a signal was just before they entered town. So her phone must have been switched off... or destroyed."

"Now why would she do a thing like that?" asked Chase, more to himself than to the rest of us. "Unless they ran into some unsavory types who destroyed her cell phone and took the RV off the road."

"Let's go out there tomorrow and see what we can find," Odelia suggested.

Chase nodded. "I've got the rest of the week off, so let's make good use of the time we have, and get to the bottom of this mystery."

She gave him a smile and placed a tender hand on his arm. "I'm so glad we're doing this together, babe."

"Me too," said Chase, returning her smile and placing his

own hand on top of his wife's. They shared a loving kiss, as witnessed by Brutus and Harriet, who chose that exact moment to enter the house through the pet flap.

Brutus stared at the couple, looking distinctly perturbed, and Harriet even gasped in shock. I guess they'd never seen a loving couple before.

"Odelia, what are you doing!" Harriet cried, aghast.

"Kissing my husband," said Odelia with a smile. "Why?"

"But..." She gulped, as she directed a quick glance at Brutus, then shook her head. "No, no. It's totally fine. Just... surprising, I guess. Under the circumstances."

"A girl is missing, Harriet," I said. "But that doesn't mean life can't go on for the rest of us." It's a hard fact of life, of course, but there you have it. Even though bad things happen to people, the world keeps on turning.

"Yes," said Harriet hesitantly. "Yes, of course."

"Max, I have a message for you from Rupert," said Brutus.

I thought he was acting just as weird as Harriet was, but figured their dog training wasn't going according to schedule.

"Rupert?" I asked, getting up from my perch on the couch and sliding down to the floor. I stretched and yawned. "Who's Rupert?"

"A snail. He says you saved his life this morning."

"Oh, that's right," I said. "So what's the message?"

But Brutus was gawping at Odelia and Chase for some reason.

"Brutus? You said you had a message for me from Rupert?"

"Oh, um... Yeah, that's right. The blue moon thing is happening tonight."

I stared at my friend. "So?"

"That's the message."

"There's a blue moon out tonight?"

"Yep. He said he could smell it."

"Okay. Good to know, I guess."

"Hey, don't look at me. I'm just the messenger."

"So how is the dog training going?" I asked.

Harriet, at whom I'd directed this question, was staring at Odelia, open-mouthed, so I had to repeat my question to draw her attention.

"Oh, that's off," she said finally.

"Off? What do you mean, off?"

"Rufus proved to be a non-starter, and Fifi wants to go it alone, so the training is off."

"But…"

"Look, don't you think we have bigger fish to fry right now, Max!" she suddenly shouted, giving me a vehement look.

"Yes," I said quickly, taken aback by such vehemence. "Yes, of course."

"Well, then," she snapped, and turned on her heel. Before she exited through the pet flap, she turned back one last time. "I blame you, you know. If you hadn't taken your eye off the ball, this would never have happened!" Then she was gone.

I turned to Brutus for an explanation for this outburst, but he merely smiled weakly. "I don't blame you, Max," he said. "I mean, we all know what humans are like, don't we? Fickle. Hard to know what they'll do next." Then he was off, too.

"Fickle," I murmured. Well, that was certainly true. And the same thing could be said about certain cats.

But since the meeting was still in full swing, I decided not to pursue the matter any further, and join the conversation once more.

CHAPTER 17

"We have to do something, Brutus," said Harriet. "We have to make Odelia end this affair with her billionaire."

"But why? I thought you said you wanted to go and live with this billionaire in his castle?"

"I know what I said," she snapped. "But I gave the matter some more thought, and it stands to reason that Edward Dexter will want his new bride to live with him in San Francisco. Which means leaving Hampton Cove and all of our friends behind. And being rich and living in a castle is one thing, but I'll miss our dear friends." And of course her budding career as cat choir's number one soprano.

"But what can we do?" asked Harriet's mate. "You know she won't listen to us."

"I know," said Harriet. "But she does listen to Max. So if we can convince him to use his influence, we might still be able to turn this whole thing around."

"Max will have already talked to her, and obviously it hasn't done us any good."

"No, you're right. What I don't understand is how he can

stay so calm about it. Doesn't he realize this is going to be the end of an era for us?"

"Or the beginning of an even better one," Brutus ventured. "If only Odelia can talk her future husband into settling down in Hampton Cove instead."

She stared at her boyfriend. "Now there's an idea."

"If Ed Dexter moves to Hampton Cove, we'll all live the dream, sugar puss."

"And so we would, snuggle pooh," she said, nodding slowly.

It was true, of course, that the Pooles had always treated them very well, but imagine living in one of those million-dollar mansions on the beach, with a nice ocean view, and a helipad to take you shopping in Manhattan. Or a private jet to take you to Paris, London and Milan for Fashion Week? Now that would be the kind of life a princess like her deserved. The life she'd always dreamed of, in fact.

"You know, Brutus? Maybe we shouldn't say anything. Just let the chips fall where they may."

"It's what I would suggest," said Brutus with a grin. "And let's hope they fall in Dexter's favor—and ours!"

"Poor Chase, though. He's going to feel bad when Odelia kicks him out of the house."

"Maybe he can keep on living here for the time being. Or Dexter could buy him a small apartment in town. He'll always be Grace's dad, after all."

"Or Chase could live over Dexter's garage—take care of his fleet of fancy cars. And then Max and Dooley can stay with him. That way he won't feel so alone."

"Great idea," said Brutus, his grin widening. "Max and Dooley can keep him company, and in the meantime Odelia will have us."

"And then we'll be the ones cracking her mysteries for

her, and assisting her in writing her articles," said Harriet, who could see their future life very vividly now.

"Family parties are going to be awkward, though. Unless the Pooles disinvite Chase."

"Or Odelia decides to make a clean break and cuts off her family," said Harriet.

They shared a look of concern, then shook their heads. "Nah," said Brutus. "That would be too much, even for a billionaire's wife. It would give a bad impression."

And it was with roseate dreams of the princess life that Harriet tripped into the house to see what Marge had dropped into her bowl.

When she saw it was plain old kibble, she made a face. Always the same kibble. Good thing that soon she'd be eating from golden plates, and snacking on the best pâté money could buy. Finally the good life for her!

※

Marge wasn't in a good mood. First there was that minor snail infestation, which she could have resolved by employing some drastic measures in the form of a pesticide, but didn't want to, on account of the fact that it was bad for the soil, not to mention potentially harmful for her cats. Then there was this business with the landscaper Tex kept harping on about, no doubt pushed by their neighbor.

And now Odelia having an affair with Edward Dexter!

If she hadn't seen the pictures she wouldn't have believed the story. Not Odelia, just about the most sensible woman on the planet. And as far as she could tell, still firmly smitten with her husband. Then again, like Tex said, you never know what happens in a marriage. Maybe they'd been fighting, and hadn't told anyone. It often happens that

PURRFECT SLUG

when a baby enters the picture, it changes the dynamic between a couple, and sometimes leads to a relationship breakdown.

But this? This was simply tragic.

And so she heaved a deep sigh as she sat at her kitchen table and nursed a cup of hot chamomile tea, which never failed to soothe those frayed nerves. It didn't do a lot for her tonight, though. And when Harriet plaintively said that she was sick and tired of eating the same old kibble day in and day out, she had a good mind to work out her frustration on the prissy Persian.

Instead, she opened a can of wet food and dumped its contents into Harriet's bowl.

Moments later, the cat was snacking away to her heart's content.

At least one member of the family still had their appetite. She hadn't been able to eat a single bite of food during dinner, with Tex droning on about some cheap and reputable landscaper he found on Craigslist, and Ma making all kinds of wild suggestions about the family intervention they were planning to set up.

She glanced up at the big clock on the wall. It was coming up on eight o'clock. Time to get going.

Just then, Dooley wandered into the kitchen through the pet flap, and took up position in front of her on the floor.

"Marge?" said Dooley.

She looked up. "Mh?"

"Is snail slime bad for you?"

She frowned. Now where did that come from? "I don't think so," she said.

"It's just that the backyard is full of slimy trails from all of those snails, and Harriet says snail slime might be toxic to cats, and I hope she's wrong, cause every time we go out there I get the stuff all over myself, and then I have to lick it off." He gave her a worried look. "So you're saying it's safe, even when ingested?"

"I'm sure snail slime isn't toxic, Dooley," she said with a smile, but then his words seemed to penetrate. "What do you mean, the backyard is full of snails?"

"Well, there has been a lot of snail activity lately," said the small fluffy cat, "but tonight they seem to be extra active. They're everywhere now."

"Oh, dear," she said, and got up to take a look. She ventured out through the kitchen door, and discovered to her dismay Dooley was right. There were snails pretty much all over the backyard. They were crawling on the lawn, covering her precious flowers, and the bushes were absolutely infested with them.

"This is getting worse and worse," she said.

Next door, Marcie's head came poking over the hedge. "Snail infestation, huh?" said the woman.

"Is it the same over on your side?" asked Marge.

"We've got a couple of them, but nothing like you got," said Marcie. "But they're bound to head into our backyard soon, so if I were you, I'd do something about it, and do it quick. Unless you want to get in trouble with your neighbors."

She nodded as she stepped over a couple of snails examining the porch, and joined Marcie at the hedge.

"I don't understand," she said. "We never had this problem before, and now all of a sudden they're literally everywhere."

"Maybe it's something in the soil? Or have you left your garbage out? Snails do love garbage. Can't get enough of it."

"No, we didn't leave anything out."

Marcie gave her a keen look. "I couldn't help but overhear you and Tex talking about Odelia this afternoon. Is it true? Is she having an affair with Edward Dexter, the billionaire?"

"I'm afraid so," said Marge sadly. "My mother found out quite by accident, and now we don't know what to do."

"If I were you I'd confront her about it," said Marcie. "Make her see the error of her ways, so to speak. Point out that she has a good husband in Chase."

"The best."

"Like you say, the best. And a child to consider. Now I can understand why a woman would stumble into an affair with a billionaire. Lord knows we've all secretly indulged in the fantasy. But that's just what it is: a fantasy. If she leaves her family for that man, she's going to regret it for the rest of her life."

"I know," said Marge. "Which is why we're staging an intervention. Try to talk some sense into her. Though I'm afraid we're too late already."

"She is stubborn," Marcie agreed. "Always was, even as a child."

Marge nodded, thinking back to the time when Odelia had gotten it into her head that she was going to be a vegan from now on, and had stuck to her guns no matter what. The upshot had been that the whole family had turned vegan for a while, which had been an interesting episode, until Odelia had discovered that her grandmother snuck out of the house every night to visit their local Burger King. At which point the little girl had joined her, and before long Marge and Tex were the only ones still adhering to a vegan lifestyle, all for the sake of their daughter.

"Look, can I give you one piece of advice?" said Marcie, placing a hand on her neighbor's arm.

Marge nodded absentmindedly, her thoughts now elsewhere.

"Don't be too hard on her. It's probably just a phase, you know. Something to do with becoming a mother. When I had Klara I was depressed for three months, and gained about forty pounds. I'm sure Odelia's affair with this billionaire falls into the same category. She'll snap out of it, just you wait and see."

"I hope you're right," said Marge, offering her neighbor a sad smile.

"And for heaven's sake, do something about those snails!" Marcie added as she plucked a particularly large and brazen specimen from her sleeve.

CHAPTER 18

The strange phenomenon of the snail infestation clearly baffled Marge, who proceeded to shoot the breeze with her neighbor Marcie, causing Dooley and myself to return to our own backyard, carefully sidestepping dozens and dozens of these denizens of snaildom. Marge may have insisted that the slime of the common snail isn't bad for cats, but I wasn't so sure. And besides, humans aren't in the habit of ingesting whatever attaches itself to their outer crust the way cats do. We're forced to ingest and digest this slime every time we groom ourselves! And who knows what havoc it might wreak on our sensitive digestive systems.

"Do you think this has something to do with that blue moon business?" asked Dooley.

"What blue moon business?" I asked as I balanced precariously on three legs while trying to avoid a cluster of snails that had crossed my path.

"Well, what Rupert the snail told Brutus to tell you. The blue moon business. That tonight there is a blue moon out."

We both glanced up automatically, but since the moon

wasn't out yet, we couldn't determine whether it was going to be blue, or the regular milky white.

"I'm not sure, Dooley," I said. Frankly I'd completely forgotten about this whole blue moon business. What is a blue moon anyway? It's not as if the moon can change color. It's just a big dead chunk of rock floating in orbit around our own slightly more lively planet.

"I just wish they'd take a hike," I said. I don't mind creatures of every denomination to go about their business in peace and harmony, but too much is too much.

Tex must have thought the same, for he now came stepping through the opening in the hedge, trying not to smush a snail, and balancing on one foot as he did so, picking his way across the garden in the direction of the terrace.

"Chase!" he bellowed. "We have to do something about these snails!"

Chase, who'd been preparing dinner, now came out. He had tomato sauce all over his face, a testament to his signature dish: spaghetti bolognese, the sauce of which he claims to have perfected, even though I've seen the glass jars with tomato sauce from a popular brand lined up in the kitchen cupboard.

"What snails?" asked the cop. But then he must have seen what we all saw, for his jaw dropped a little, and he said, "Oh, those snails."

"What do you suggest?" asked Tex, planting his hands on his hips. "We can't just let them have at it. There won't be a single plant or flower left!"

"Where did they come from, all of a sudden?"

"I have no idea, but we've got to get them out of here, before they crawl into Kurt's backyard, and he sues us for spreading a harmful substance!"

Kurt, who's like a genie when you mention his name, popped up over the fence.

"If they set as much as one foot onto my private property," the retired music teacher warned, "I'm going to the cops!"

"I am the cops, Kurt," Chase reminded him calmly.

"I mean the other cops—the ones that give a damn!"

"I give a damn," said Chase. "I want to get rid of these snails as much as you."

"So why don't you just spray them?" our irate neighbor demanded. "All it takes is a gallon of slug and snail killer and you'll never see the little suckers again!"

"Because we don't want to poison our cats in the meantime, or your dog, for that matter," said Chase, as he gestured to Fifi, whose snout had just appeared in the hole she'd dug under the fence.

Kurt had to admit that perhaps Chase had a point, but he still insisted we get rid of the snail population or else!

And then he was gone again.

I joined Fifi, mostly to see how her training regimen was going, but also to inquire about the state of her own backyard.

"No, we don't have any snails," she said. "Which is strange, cause your backyard seems to be infested with them, and usually they spread out."

"Marge and Tex's backyard seems to be the center of snail attention," I said, "with our backyard enjoying a sort of spin-off effect. It's an odd phenomenon." It was true. Most of the snail activity was concentrated next door, with a few stragglers having taken up residence in Odelia and Chase's little patch of green.

"And as far as the training for the dog show is concerned," said Fifi, "I'm afraid to say it's not going well, Max. Plus, there's the fact that I need Kurt to enter me into the show, and he's not the kind of person who likes that kind of thing."

"So have you considered that Odelia might have a word with him? She might be able to convince him."

"I don't know," she said, casting a dubious glance back in the direction of her human. "He's not really in a good mood right now, what with the snail thing and all. Maybe better catch him when he's in a better mood."

"Which may be never," I told her gently.

She grimaced. "Yeah, I guess you're right. He's never anything but kind to me, you know. Which is weird, cause he's never anything but mean to other humans."

"Some people are like that," I said. "They hate other people, but they love their pets and would do anything for them. Which is why he might be convinced to let you enter that show. If he thinks you would enjoy it."

"Okay, let's give it a shot," she said, well pleased.

"Oh, and Harriet has given up training Rufus, so you might join him for his training activities again. I have a feeling he'd improve a lot quicker when you and he work together as a team."

She gave me a warm smile. "You're a wise cat, Max, has anyone ever told you that?"

"Oh, well," I murmured with a touch of embarrassment. "Just trying to help."

"Now look what these crazy humans of yours are doing," said Fifi with a chuckle.

I glanced back, and saw that Chase and Tex were picking up the snails one by one, and depositing them into plastic buckets.

"What are they doing?" I asked.

"I think they're going to forcefully evict them," said Dooley. "At least I heard Chase say something about an eviction notice."

It was one way to handle the situation, of course. But judging by the sheer number of snails, it was also a very slow process!

CHAPTER 19

The spectacle was perhaps a strange one, but Marge figured her husband and son-in-law probably had a point, so she took the plastic tub that she usually reserved for the laundry, and started collecting snails as well.

"Where are we going to put them?" she asked.

"Back there," her husband gestured. "In the field."

Stretching behind the backyards of all the houses on Harrington Street, a field lay. It belonged to Blake Carrington, who let the field lie fallow, and had spurned many offers from real estate developers to turn it into expensive apartments.

And so the snail harvesting proceeded. And when Ma arrived, and joined in, and Odelia as well, and even Marge's brother Alec and his girlfriend Charlene, who often dropped by for dinner, between the seven of them they progressed nicely.

"If we keep this up we'll have de-snailed this whole place in no time!" said Tex excitedly. He'd taken the role of coordinator upon himself, since it was his idea in the first place, and was having a blast.

Chase and Odelia were working side by side, and judging from their laughing and occasionally planting a snail in the other person's neck, didn't seem like a quarreling couple at all.

Ma saw her looking in Odelia's direction, and sidled up to her.

"Maybe we don't need to stage an intervention," the old lady suggested. "Maybe things will work out all by themselves for once."

"Yeah, I think you're right. Just look at them. Does that look like a couple in trouble?"

"Maybe she dropped this billionaire guy already. Could be that it was just a fling," said Ma. "A momentary lapse of judgment."

"Yeah, a moment of weakness and now she's forgotten all about it. Would be a pity for us to drag it all up again."

"Let's can the intervention idea for the present. And let's get rid of the snails!"

The captured snails were all released on the far side of Blake Carrington's field, from which hopefully they wouldn't return. Plenty of food for them there.

Finally the work was done, and all of them stood regarding their now snail-free backyards with distinct pride.

"And now let's eat!" said Ma. "I'm starving!"

"What's for dinner?" asked Alec.

"Escargot," Chase quipped.

And as they sat down for dinner, Marge watched her family tuck into Chase's spaghetti bolognese with an uplifted heart. Looked like all was well after all.

"Poor snails," said Dooley as we watched the proceedings from the porch swing. "Now they have to crawl all the way back here."

"Do you think they'll come back?" I asked.

"Of course they will," said Brutus. "Snails are very difficult to get rid of. They will keep coming back again, once they've sampled your wares."

"It's far, though, isn't it?" asked Dooley. "From all the way out in the field?"

"It might take them a couple of hours, but mark my words," said Brutus. "They will be back."

Which made me wonder why that was. What was so appealing about this particular place that they'd spend hours crawling along, passing perfectly edible greenery, just to have another whack at Tex and Marge's little garden of delight?

I would have asked them, if I had the chance, but all the snails I'd encountered had been of the strong silent type, and had simply ignored me. And of Rupert there was no sign.

"Looks like Odelia and Chase have patched things up," Harriet remarked casually.

"Patched what up?" I asked.

"Did they have a fight?!" Dooley asked.

"Worse," said Harriet. "Much worse."

"Odelia is having an affair!" said Brutus.

"An affair!" Dooley cried, then considered Brutus's words. "What affair?"

"An affair with a billionaire," said Brutus. "But why are you asking us all these questions? You know what happened. According to Gran you were right there when they were schmoozing in that restaurant."

"Yeah, we saw the pictures," said Harriet.

"What restaurant? What billionaire?" I asked.

"Oh, Max, don't be like that," said Harriet with an eyeroll. "You don't have to protect Odelia, all right? It's us! You can tell us what happened."

"Did they go upstairs after kissing and fondling in that restaurant?" asked Brutus. "Did they go up to his suite?"

"Look, I have no idea what you're talking about," I said. "All I know is that Odelia had a meeting with Edward Dexter in the bar of the Star Hotel. Edward's daughter Addie has gone missing, and he asked Odelia to find her. There was no kissing, no fondling, no schmoozing, and she certainly didn't go up to his suite."

A stunned silence ensued, then Harriet asked, "But what about the pictures?"

"What pictures?" I said, not bothering to hide a touch of exasperation.

"Gran took a bunch of pictures of Odelia and her billionaire hugging and kissing."

"She even shot a video!" said Brutus, as if this was the deciding argument.

"Odelia may have hugged Mr. Dexter at some point, since she felt for the man, as he's worried that something very bad happened to his daughter, and it's possible that Gran caught this moment, but it was an entirely amicable hug, and nothing untoward happened," I said.

More silence followed, and finally Brutus shrugged. "You know what they say. No smoke without fire. So something must have happened."

"Nothing happened!" I said. "And I would know, because—as you've already indicated—I was right there!"

"You wouldn't be lying to us, now would you, Max?" said Harriet, giving me a suspicious look.

"No, Harriet, I would not," I said.

"Poor Mr. Dexter," said Dooley. "He had such high hopes

for his daughter, and instead she decided to become a juggler in a circus."

"Oh, Dooley," I said with a sigh.

CHAPTER 20

The hour was late, and so the time had come to visit cat choir. I would have stayed home, and tried to find out more about this blue moon business, but since there were no snails left, and the ones I'd asked what Rupert could possibly mean, had given me the cold shoulder treatment, I decided to put the matter to bed, so to speak, and focus my attention elsewhere.

We still had a missing girl to find, and her equally missing boyfriend, and I was hoping that my friends at cat choir might be able to point me in the right direction as far as the search effort was concerned.

"Did you know that Odelia was having an affair, Max?" asked Dooley.

"No, I did not, Dooley," I said. "For the simple reason that Odelia is not having an affair."

"She's not?"

"No, of course not. Why in heaven's name would she want to have an affair with a billionaire?"

Okay, scratch that. Having an affair with a billionaire is probably very high on the wish list of many persons of the female persuasion. But since Odelia is a happily married woman, and a new mother, I didn't think she was even remotely interested in this Dexter fellow. Though he may have touched a chord when he almost burst into tears. But that didn't mean she was going to throw herself into his arms and stroke his hair and give him sweet kisses to make the pain go away.

"I think she wanted to have an affair, but she saw that Gran was watching her," said Harriet, "and so she stopped herself before things went too far."

I had to stop *myself* from making a comment, and so I did. No sense in getting into an argument.

"And I think she didn't want to have an affair in front of Max and Dooley," said Brutus.

"But why?" asked Dooley.

"Because it wouldn't be proper," said Harriet primly. "And also, she would probably feel self-conscious."

"What do you mean?" asked Dooley.

"Well, you know how it is. You don't like to do your business in front of another cat, do you?" asked Harriet.

Dooley didn't seem to get the picture. "I don't know," he said. "I don't really care, I guess. All I care about is that everything comes out the way it should."

"Okay, so you're the exception to the rule," said Harriet with a touch of annoyance. "But take it from me, humans don't wash their dirty laundry in public."

"But... why would Odelia want to wash her laundry in front of Mr. Dexter? Or do her business?"

"You're deliberately misinterpreting my words, aren't you, Dooley?" said Harriet, getting worked up. "What I said was—"

"I think we know what you said," I said.

"And I don't think you do!"

"Let's just put the matter to bed," I suggested.

"All right, fine. But for his own edification, I think it's important that Dooley understands what's been going on right under his own nose!"

Dooley went cross-eyed for a moment, trying to look at his own nose. "My nose is fine," he announced finally. "At least I think it is. Can you look at my nose and tell me if you see anything unusual, Max?"

"Your nose is fine, Dooley," I said. "Look, I think we can all agree that Odelia would never hook up with this billionaire," I added. "She loves Chase, he loves her, and they just had a baby together. They're happy, and there's absolutely no reason for her to get involved with anyone else."

"I can give you a billion reasons," said Brutus with a grin.

"Odelia isn't like that," I said. "She doesn't care how much money a person has in the bank."

"No, I guess not," said Harriet, and for the first time that night I noticed how unhappy she looked. And then I understood.

"You wanted the story of this affair to be true, didn't you?" I said. "You wanted to go and live with this billionaire guy."

"And what if I did? Life as a billionaire's cat must be fantastic."

"I think we have a pretty great life already," I said, giving her a slightly reproachful look. "And what happened to being grateful for what you have?"

"I am grateful, don't get me wrong," said Harriet. "But I would be even more grateful if we had, you know, more."

"More of what?" asked Dooley, interested.

"More of everything! More food, more space, more toys. I'm a princess, you guys. And a princess needs her creature comforts."

And so she does, and I actually felt for Harriet. Always wanting more. Must be tough.

We'd arrived at the park, where cat choir gets together of an evening, and I saw that the playground was packed already, which meant we were late.

Shanille didn't seem to mind, though. She's cat choir's conductor, and the one who keeps us cats in check, to some extent.

"So is it true?" she asked the moment she spotted us.

"Is what true?" I asked, puzzled.

"Well, that you're all going to go and live with Edward Dexter, of course!"

"No, it's not true," I said.

"It might be true," said Harriet. "Odelia only has to say the word, and we could all be living like royalty."

"She's not going to say the word," I reiterated my earlier point.

"What word would this be?" asked Dooley.

"From what I heard Odelia was seen kissing with Mr. Dexter," said Kingman, another one of our dear friends. "In fact they were kissing so much the windows of his electric car were all steamed up."

"They were not in an electric car and no windows were steamed up," I said with a sigh.

"They could have been steamed up," said Harriet. "In fact they could still be steamed up, if only Odelia wants them to be."

"She doesn't," I said.

"What windows would this be?" asked Dooley.

"I like Edward Dexter," said Shanille. "He's going to make us all go electric."

"And shoot us into space," said Kingman.

"But I don't want to be shot into space!" Dooley cried, alarmed.

"Too bad, Dooley," said Brutus with a grin. "You don't get

a say in the matter, I'm afraid. Before you know it, we'll all be living on Mars. Or the Moon. I'm not sure which."

"But I don't want to live on the Moon!"

"Tough luck, buddy."

Dooley turned to me. "Tell Odelia not to say the word, Max, and let Mr. Dexter steam up her windows, otherwise we'll have to fly to the Moon!"

"Don't listen to these cats, Dooley," I said, shooting a disapproving look at Brutus and the others, who now stood shaking with laughter at my friend's distress. "They're all talking out of their behinds."

And I placed a paw on Dooley's shoulder and led him away.

"How do you talk out of your behind, Max? I didn't even know that was possible."

"It's a tough trick to master, Dooley," I said. "And it works better for some than for others. But Brutus does it better than anyone I know." And with these words, I directed a final critical glance at Dooley's tormentor, but Brutus merely gave me a grin in return and even shook his patootie at me!

Some cats have a lot of nerve.

CHAPTER 21

I still hadn't found what I was looking for, but then I spotted the very cat I'd come there to see. Frédérique is a very pretty red cat of unknown descent, who lives with the man who runs the gas station, located on the main road between Happy Bays and Hampton Cove. It's a very popular gas station, and Mel Corset, the man who owns it, has been running it for many years.

"Frédérique," I said, approaching the tiny redhead. "Exactly the cat I need."

She'd been licking her tail, and now looked up, clearly surprised. "Me?"

"Yes, you," I said. "We're conducting an important investigation, and I'm hoping you might be able to help us."

She stared at me, wide-eyed. "Are you sure you mean me?"

"Yes, I mean you," I confirmed.

"Oh, boy," she said, suddenly looking extremely bashful. "Oh, boy, oh, boy, oh, boy."

"Why do you keep saying 'Oh, boy?'" asked Dooley, intrigued by Frédérique's speech pattern.

"Because it's not every day that the great Max needs my help," she said, eyeing me from beneath lowered lashes.

"I wouldn't exactly call myself great," I said.

"Oh, but you are," she assured me. "I've been following your adventures with great interest, Max. How you always manage to get your guy. It's uncanny."

"I get a lot of help," I said, referring to my friend, who was eyeing Frédérique with marked curiosity.

"It's his head," said Dooley now. "It's very big."

"Thank you, Dooley," I murmured.

"It has to be big, for his big brain to fit," Dooley continued. "And then because his head is so big and heavy, he needs a big neck, and also a big body, otherwise his head would fall down all the time. Which is why Max is as big as he is. And why he's so successful at what he does. It's all to do with his bigness."

"Yes, Dooley, I think we get the picture."

"I don't think Max is big," said Frédérique. "I think he's just the right size. Very butch, and very brave, too, to be fighting crime like he does."

"Well, thank you, Frédérique," I said, "but..."

"And he must be very clever. So clever that he can outsmart any villain."

"That's very kind of you," I said, trying to get a word in edgewise.

"In fact I think he's probably the smartest cat that ever lived, and it's an honor for me to finally be able to assist you, Max." She stared at me fervently, and I would have wondered if a feverish blush was mantling her cheek, but with all of that hair it was hard to know for sure.

"Okay, so the thing is that two weeks ago a woman passed through town with her boyfriend, and they've since vanished from the face of the earth."

"Joined a circus," Dooley intimated.

"They were traveling in an RV and the last place they were seen was at your human's gas station. They were heading in this direction, and the final signal from her phone came from the road just outside of town, so—"

"You want me to help you look for her. Join the gang. How cool!" said Frédérique with pretty excitement.

"Well, no, but I do want you to think back, and maybe to remember if you saw that RV, and perhaps any details of the transaction that you can remember."

"You don't want me to help you track down this woman?"

"I think we're fine for the tracking," I said with a smile, "but we do need more information about what happened when she pulled into the gas station."

Frédérique frowned, and set herself to searching her memory. Finally she must have hit upon something, for she brightened. "I think I've got it!" she announced excitedly. "I did see an RV. It was bright pink, and there was a family inside. A woman, a man, a little boy, another little boy, and two girls—twins!" She sat beaming at me, as if she'd just performed the greatest trick in the world.

"Um... how old were this man and this woman?"

"Oh, I don't know. You know how hard it is to know for sure how old humans are."

"Take a guess," I suggested.

"Okay, so, like, maybe a hundred? Or two hundred?"

I heaved a mental sigh. "Addie and her boyfriend were traveling alone, as far as we know, and they have no kids, since they're practically kids themselves. She just graduated from college, and so did Ted Machosko, her boyfriend."

"Oh," said Frédérique, visibly disappointed. Then all of a sudden she burst into tears. "Oh, Max! I was trying to help you but I failed! I'm so, so sorry!"

"It's all right," I said, patting her on the back. "You did your best."

"It's just that so many of these RVs pass through town, especially in the tourist season, it's hard to keep track!"

"No, I'm sure you're right," I said. I hadn't taken into account that traveling in an RV is a very popular pastime, and possibly hundreds of these vehicles pull into Mel Corset's gas station every month, possibly even every couple of days, since the Hamptons are very popular as a tourist destination.

"Look, tell you what we'll do. We'll talk to your human tomorrow, and hopefully he'll have a camera and recording equipment, and maybe he'll have caught the RV on tape. And then I want you to keep an eye on him during our visit, and also later on, and when you notice anything suspicious, I want you to tell me. Do you think you can do that?"

She nodded about sixty times in quick succession, drying her eyes in the process. "Yes, Max. I'll do that for you. I'll keep a close eye on Mel and I'll tell you if he acts suspiciously." Then she reconsidered. "Only... how do I know he's acting suspiciously?"

"Well... if he talks to someone on the phone about that RV, for instance, or if he suddenly acts different."

"Okay, yes, I think I can do that," she confirmed, and gave me a look of determination. "Frédérique at your service! Consider me part of Team Max!" And to prove she wasn't kidding, she stood up straight, and gave me a salute by placing her paw against her forehead. "Frédérique is Team Max all the way!" she cried.

"At ease, soldier," I murmured, and removed myself from the scene before things got too awkward.

"Why would Frédérique's human behave suspiciously, Max?" asked Dooley.

"Just a hunch, Dooley. If that gas station was the last place where Addie was seen, the guy who owns it might have had something to do with her disappearance, wouldn't you say?"

He gave me a look of admiration. "Good thinking, Max!"

"Just using the old noggin," I said.

"The very big noggin," he said.

CHAPTER 22

That night, I slept like a rose at the foot of Odelia and Chase's bed. And even though Grace woke us all up from time to time, as she does, it was still a peaceful night in every respect. The moon filtered faintly in through the curtains, and if it was blue, I certainly didn't notice. As far as I could tell, it looked just about the same as every other night. Then again, cats do have trouble seeing certain colors, and so maybe that might have had something to do with it.

When morning broke, and I got up, feeling refreshed and ready for a new day, I saw to my satisfaction that our humans were still fast asleep, and they were even cuddling, a clear testament to the complete nonsensicality of Gran's claims that Odelia would have fallen into the arms of that billionaire.

But before I could close my eyes for one of those pleasant after-naps, a sudden cry of anguish rent the air, and had us all up and about in next to no time. For I think we'd all recognized that anguished cry as coming from next door, and belonging to none other than Odelia's father Tex!

Chase was the first one to hammer down the stairs, with

PURRFECT SLUG

Odelia a close second, and Dooley and myself bringing up the rear.

"What do you think happened, Max?" asked Dooley, but then we had to step aside, for Odelia was stomping back up the stairs to pick Grace from her crib and bring her along.

"I have no idea, but whatever it is, it must be bad," I said.

Judging from the sound of Tex's voice, he must have either hit his toe, or poked himself in the eye, or fallen prey to some other terrible fate!

We all hurried into the next-door garden, and I must say that the scene that met our eyes was a harrowing one indeed!

Tex was there, on hands and knees, bent over the remnants of a small bush, and when I say remnants I do mean remnants: not a single leaf was left on that particular bush, and when I looked a little closer, I saw that there was not a single leaf left anywhere in that entire garden. And not a single flower either. It almost seemed as if some giant hand had come down overnight, and had rummaged around a little, destroying every living organism!

Well, not every organism, for the garden was completely infested with... snails.

I could see hundreds of them, perhaps even thousands, and they were still busy chewing on everything they could find, even blades of grass!

"My garden!" Tex howled. "They destroyed my garden!"

Marge had also descended from her room, clad in a nightgown, and stood eyeing the scene with a pensive expression on her face.

"So they came back," said Chase, as he picked up a snail and studied it for a moment, then put it back, wiping his hand on his boxers.

Suddenly a window was thrown open upstairs, and Gran appeared. "What's with the racket!" she demanded. "Do you know how hard it is to fall asleep at my age? Oh..." She'd also seen what had happened, and her face sort of sagged. "Oh, no," she muttered. "Who did this!"

"Snails," said Marge simply.

"Not those snails again!" said the old lady, shaking her fist. "I thought we got rid of those pests!"

"They came back," said Tex, stating the obvious.

"Unless these are different snails," said Dooley, and there was a certain logic in what he said.

Brutus and Harriet came trudging out of the house, jaws moving and the look of two contented cats who'd just eaten their fill on their faces.

"Oh, look," said Brutus. "More snails."

"I thought you got rid of them?" asked Harriet.

"We did get rid of them," said Marge.

"I think it's different ones," Dooley intimated. "These are probably distant cousins twice removed, who decided to drop in for a visit."

"And I think it's the same ones," I said, cause they were giving me the same cold-shoulder treatment as the ones last night had done.

Next door, two heads popped up over the hedge: they belonged to Ted and Marcie Trapper.

"Oh, my God," said Ted. "What happened here, neighbor?"

"Snails," said Tex curtly, his customary geniality a thing of the past. "They destroyed my garden."

"Our garden," Marge corrected him. "How about you, Ted? Did they also attack your plants?"

"No, over here everything is hunky-dory," said Ted cheerfully. "And a good thing, too, otherwise I'd have to sue you, Tex." He grinned. "Just kidding."

"I don't get it," said Odelia. "Why do they keep coming back here? Why this particular garden?"

"Yeah, what's so special about your garden?" asked Ted,

scratching his scalp. "Are you spraying something, Tex? Or using some special fertilizer or something?"

Tex shook his head. "Just plenty of TLC," he said brokenly. "And endless patience."

"Pity Rupert isn't here," said Dooley. "He might know the answer."

"Yeah, I don't see him around," I said. "And this lot isn't talking, that's for sure."

"Like thieves in the night," Harriet scoffed. "At least thieves have the decency to remove themselves from the scene of the crime."

She was right. These snails were staying put, even though they'd already reduced the garden to a wasteland. So why weren't they shifting?

"Could it be the blue moon?" asked Dooley.

"Could be," I said. Though what the moon had to do with anything was beyond me.

There was a sort of commotion or scuffle when Tex had to be restrained by his wife and son-in-law. "So help me God I'm going to kill them all!" the usually mild-mannered doctor was screaming. "I'm going to dump a ton of pesticide on top of them!"

"No, Dad," said Odelia. "Don't do it."

"Yeah, don't do it, Tex," said Ted. "That poison will seep into the ground and then my garden will also be affected."

"Our garden," said Marcie dryly, as she exchanged a look of understanding with Marge. Boys and their toys, that look seemed to say.

"Maybe this time we'll consult a specialist," said Marge, patting her disconsolate husband on the back. "And maybe he'll be able to get rid of this pest."

"See?" said Ted. "What did I tell you, Tex? We need to bring in a professional. It's the only way to go."

But Tex merely nodded, then slumped off in the direction of the house.

"Looks like those snails broke the camel's back," said Chase, shaking his head.

Dooley opened his mouth to speak, but I held up a paw. It wasn't the right time to discuss the similarities between Tex and a camel.

CHAPTER 23

Mel Corset proved most helpful, which probably was a given, since he'd made it his life's work to help others by filling up their gas tanks and providing those little extras like clean windshields and oil to lubricate their engines.

"Of course I have a security camera," he said when Chase informed him that we were trying to locate a certain vehicle on a certain day at a certain time. "You can never be too careful these days. You'd be amazed how many people try to take off without paying. Now what day did you say you wanted me to look at?"

We proceeded to a back room located behind the counter, where a series of recorders stood humming away with industrious diligence. Behind Mr. Corset's counter a bank of screens provided him with a good overview of the goings-on at his gas station, and the little shop attached to it, but back here all of those images were also recorded on a set of sturdy disks, and kept for posterity.

"How long do you keep the recordings?" asked Chase, not hiding his admiration for the man's setup.

"Indefinitely," said Mel proudly. "You never know if at some point in the near or far future a cop will drop by, just like you're doing now, and ask me if I've got the recordings for some date far in the past, like you're doing now. And then it's an honor and a privilege for me to be able to tell him, like I'm telling you now: of course I've got that footage for you, officer, like I'm about to show you now."

And he dug into a large metal filing cabinet, where a series of discs were neatly lined up, organized according to date.

"Here we go," said Mel, as he handed Chase a disk. "This should do the trick."

"Where can I watch this?" asked Chase.

"Oh, you can take it, if you want. I keep copies of everything you see in here. A physical copy at home, of course, and a digital copy in the cloud. You can never be too prepared or organized, just in case a cop drops by and needs a copy, like you do now." And he beamed at us with pride written all over his features.

On our way out, I noticed Frédérique studying her human carefully, only taking a break from her intense scrutiny to give me a wink.

I gave her two thumbs up. If Mel Corset was involved in the disappearance of Addie Dexter and Ted Machosko, Frédérique would find out and let us know.

Our next port of call was the police precinct, where Chase had the setup needed to study the security footage more closely.

And so the long wait began. I don't know if you've ever tried to find something on CCTV footage before, but it's more or less the same thing as trying to find your glasses: the thing you want is almost always in the very last place you look. Not that cats wear glasses, of course. Our eyesight is perfect, thank you very much.

PURRFECT SLUG

And as Chase and Odelia studied the cars as they passed through the gas station, hoping to catch a glimpse of Addie and her boyfriend, Dooley and I wandered through the police precinct, hoping to find a bite to eat. A very nice officer must have understood our predicament, for she very kindly provided us with a plate with some pieces of meatball on it.

"Meatball," said Dooley after we'd dug in. "Yum."

"I still wonder why those snails all descended on Tex and Marge's garden like that," I said.

"Do you think snail tastes like meatball?" asked Dooley, chewing noisily.

"I have no idea, Dooley, and I don't intend to find out."

"I think they taste like snot," said my friend. "Slimy, you know."

"Let's not talk about snot while we're eating," I suggested.

"Max, Dooley!" suddenly Odelia said, as she came storming into the small precinct kitchen. "We found her!"

And so they had. On the screen, when we walked back into Chase's office, a large RV was clearly visible, and as he slowed down the footage, and zoomed in, a blond-haired young woman came into view. She was walking from the RV to the gas station, presumably to pay the bill, and as she did, a second person emerged from the RV. He was dark-haired, lanky, and had sharpish features.

"I don't like him," said Dooley immediately. "I think he killed Addie and then took off."

"I thought you said she became a juggler and he became a clown?" I said.

"Now I'm thinking he probably became a knife thrower, and practiced on his girlfriend and missed."

We all studied the footage, as Chase ran it a couple of times. Finally Addie got back on board the RV, and the vehicle passed from view, traveling in the direction of Hampton Cove.

"How far did they travel before Addie's cell phone cut out?" asked Odelia.

"About another ten minutes," said Chase. "Which puts her exactly..." He'd pulled up a map on his screen, and pointed to a place just outside town. "Here."

"We better go and have a look," said Odelia as she got up.

The spot Chase had indicated was located at the foot of a steep hill that gradually turns into a densely wooded area, a place popular with hikers and people looking for some peace and quiet. There are also several log cabins in there, where nature lovers can go and enjoy some time away from civilization. And when you keep traveling like the crow flies, there's a lake where supposedly the fishing is good. But since it's hard to find, and even harder to reach—there are no roads that lead up there—fortunately for the fish not many people get that far.

"Let's hope Addie isn't buried in those woods," said Chase as he pulled on his jacket. "Because we might never find her."

"Let's think positive," Odelia suggested. "She might still be alive."

But her words lacked the ring of conviction.

CHAPTER 24

I don't know what Chase had hoped to find, but when we got to the approximate location where Addie's phone had transmitted its final signal, there wasn't much of interest to see.

"Mh," said Chase, as he stood on the side of the road, staring into the woods.

"No RV?" asked Dooley.

"No RV," I said. Which was probably too much to hope for, after all.

"See? I told you: she joined a traveling..." When I gave him a look of censure, he quickly amended, "... band."

"Of course she did."

"I don't suppose Randal Skip ever searched these woods?" asked Chase.

"No, I don't suppose he did."

Chase placed a hand to his eyes to shield them from a sun that was beating down on us. "It would take days to comb this area, even if we had the manpower." He suddenly crouched down, looking intently at the road. "Look at this."

"What is it?"

"I'll bet this is where that RV went off the road."

There were indeed tire marks that led off the road and onto the shoulder.

"You think Addie and Ted had an accident?" asked Odelia

"Either an accident or they were deliberately run off the road."

"How can you be so sure?"

"Cause this doesn't look like the tire tracks of an ordinary vehicle. These tracks were made by a much heavier vehicle, like an RV."

"Could be a truck. Could be anything."

"Sure. But taken in conjunction with the information we have about that cell phone signal, there's a good chance their RV met with an accident right here. And if you think about it: why would her phone suddenly die on her like that?"

"Maybe it got damaged in the accident?"

"Or it was smashed up by whoever drove them off the road," said Chase grimly.

"I don't like this, Max," said Dooley. "Chase is making it sound as if something terrible happened to Addie."

"That's because he's a cop, Dooley," I said. "He's programmed to think the worst, given his experience."

"So you think Addie might still be alive?"

"Yes, of course. There could be any number of reasons why that phone died. Like a battery malfunction, or, like Chase said, it got smashed up in an accident."

"If her phone got smashed up, chances are that Addie got smashed up, too," Dooley argued. "Kids these days have those phones practically glued to their hands."

He was right, of course. If Addie's phone was dead, there was a good chance that so was that phone's owner. But we owed it to Mr. Dexter to take a positive view of the situation, and until we found a body, we had to work from the assumption that his daughter was still alive somewhere.

But if she was, why hadn't she been in touch? Why had this accident Chase was referring to not been brought to the attention of the emergency services? And where was that RV now? Big vehicles like that don't just disappear.

Lots of questions, and no answers. But at least we had a place where we could start looking for the missing couple.

"We're going to need more people," said Chase. "Lots and lots more people."

"Edward doesn't want more people brought in," Odelia reminded him.

"We can't possibly cover these woods between the two of us, babe."

"No, I know," said Odelia, and that's when she glanced down at me!

I swallowed. "Hi, Odelia," I said, giving her a little wave with my tail.

"Max," she said, "do you think you might be able to rustle up a team of cats—and possibly dogs, too—and search these woods?"

Her request reminded me of another time we'd searched for a missing girl. Only that time we'd had suspects we'd been able to question, and at least a certainty of where the girl had disappeared. Now, for all we knew, Ted had been able to right his RV and had continued on his journey to Montauk, which meant that the couple could be anywhere now. Possibly even on their way to Florida!

But of course Odelia had a point. If a posse of pets got busy, chances were we might find some trace of the missing couple.

So I nodded my agreement. "I think I could arrange that," I said.

"Great. Then let's get busy," she said with a grateful smile. "You get as many of your friends down here as possible, and start combing this area directly in front of us, and Chase and

I will coordinate the operation from..." She searched around, until her eyes landed on a derelict sort of cowshed. She made a face. "From right there," she concluded.

"Grand HQ?" Chase grinned.

"That's right. Grand HQ between the cowpats."

"Let's get this search party going," said Chase, clapping his hands for some reason. Possibly to give himself some much-needed encouragement, for this rescue effort was going to be unusual—unorthodox, even.

Then again, what choice did we have?

And so we got busy rustling up cats!

CHAPTER 25

Getting a group of cats together is easier said than done. And getting them organized is even harder. Cats are notoriously individualistic creatures, who hate to be told what to do. And then there were the dogs, who would have to form an integral part of the team effort, if Odelia's wishes were to come true. But dogs, unlike cats, don't roam around happy and free. Most dogs are confined to their homes or kennels, or attached to their humans with something called a leash, which is to keep that human from getting lost.

But we had our orders, and carry them out, we would!

So we headed into town, where Chase would study reports of traffic accidents, and Odelia would get in touch with Edward Dexter, to give him the latest report.

Dooley and I, meanwhile, decided to go to church. No, not to pray for the wellbeing of these two young people, but to go and talk to Shanille. If there's anyone in town who has managed better than most to rally a big group of cats to form a more or less harmonious unity, it's her. I mean, if you can make dozens of cats sing in harmony, you can make them do anything!

Or at least that was the reasoning I was going with.

Okay, so I was a little desperate. Can you tell?

"You want me to do what?!" Shanille cried when we finally found her in the church garden, where she was eying a couple of birds with a distinctly malicious gleam in her eyes—not very Christian of her!

"We're looking for this couple that went missing, and since the entire operation needs to be conducted on the down-low, Odelia had the brilliant idea to involve the cats of Hampton Cove, and make them search those woods."

"And since you're the leader of Hampton Cove's cats," Dooley continued my narrative, "we thought you would be the best cat to lead us."

"You must be joking," said Shanille, though I could see she was already softening. That stuff about being a leader to cats must have made her think.

"There's only one cat in this town who can pull this off, Shanille," I said.

"And that's you," Dooley said.

"And think about Addie Dexter."

"And her poor dad."

"He's not exactly poor, is he, this billionaire of yours," Shanille sputtered. "I mean, with all the billions at his disposal, can't he employ an army to search for his daughter? Why do we have to do all the work? And besides, do you know how difficult it is to go through those woods? It could take days, or even weeks before we manage to cover that much ground."

"Odelia reckons we need to limit our search to the area between the road and the lake."

"But that's huge!"

"I know, which is why we need all the help we can get."

"All of cat choir would be a good start," said Dooley, nodding.

"Mh," said Shanille as she mulled this over.

Those birds were tweeting again, and I could tell it annoyed her to no end.

"You think this Addie Dexter is in those woods?"

"There's a big chance that she is."

"And how long has she been out there?"

"She went missing two weeks ago."

"Mh," she repeated, and did some more mulling. Finally, she said, "Okay, I'll do it. But you do realize that this girl and her boyfriend might be dead by now?"

"Of course," I said.

"We're trying to stay positive," said Dooley. "And so we like to think she's fine."

"Sounds like magical thinking to me," Shanille grumbled, causing Dooley to give me a questioning look, which I returned with a look that said, 'I'll explain it later.' First we had to get Shanille going, and going well!

The choir leader didn't disappoint, though. It had taken some effort to convince her, but once she had made her decision, she acted with... well, with decision. She started gathering her troops, and sending us to gather some more. And soon we were going house to house to get as many cats together as we could. Meeting place: the park.

Dogs were a different matter. Shanille might be a leader of cats, but she staunchly refused to also be a leader of dogs. Still, I had a remedy for that. Our secret weapon, so to speak. You see, the dogs of Hampton Cove have formed their own choir. It's not as big or as professional as cat choir, obviously, but it's expanding with leaps and bounds, so to speak. And as it happens, Fifi and Rufus are both card-carrying members of this dog choir, as they have named it.

"But we're practicing!" said Rufus when we joined him and Fifi in the backyard of Marcie and Ted.

And so they were: Rufus was standing on top of a plastic bucket, balancing on one leg, while Fifi was walking a plank, and trying not to totter into the abyss.

"A girl is missing," I said.

"And the girl's boyfriend," Dooley added.

"And it's important that we find her."

"But if we don't practice now, we'll never stand a chance!" said Rufus.

"Rufus, what's more important," said Fifi, hopping down from her plank. "The life of a missing girl, or some stupid cup?"

Rufus thought entirely too long about this simple dilemma, but finally admitted, "I don't even want a cup. I mean, where am I going to put it? I don't have a mantelpiece. Though that year's supply of kibble sounds pretty good." He directed a pleading look at Fifi, but the latter was implacable.

"We're looking for that girl," she said.

"And her boyfriend," Dooley reiterated.

"Fine," said Rufus sadly, as he stepped down from his bucket. "If you say so."

"We can practice tonight, Rufus," said Fifi. "In fact if you want we can practice all night."

"Oh, goodie," said Rufus. "I think I'm almost there. Now if I could only remember the correct sequence of the routine—that's the hard part."

And so it was that a large group of cats, and a smaller but still impressive group of dogs, gathered in the park that day. Young mothers watched this army of pets approach and grabbed their kids and skedaddled, while others snapped pictures on their phones.

And then Shanille climbed to the top of the jungle gym and cleared her throat.

It was time for her to deliver a speech.

Fire up those troops.

Tell them what was what!

"Boys and girls!" our fearless leader intoned, gesturing for the crowd to be quiet, "today marks a momentous occasion. The moment we've all been waiting for: our humans have treated us with kindness, fairness, and an abundance of kibble. Now the time has come to return the favor."

"I'm not sharing my kibble!" a cat shouted, much to the amusement of the others.

Shanille gestured for silence once more. "We're not giving them our kibble," she said, just to make matters perfectly clear from the start. "But we are giving them our time, the excellent sniffing powers of our noses, and our capacity to find what we're looking for. And if you don't know what I'm talking about: when have you dogs ever not found a buried bone?"

Loud cheers from the canine contingent greeted these words.

"And cats, when have you ever not found that last piece of kibble that managed to get wedged in behind the cupboard?"

More cheers, this time from the cats.

"And so today our humans have asked for our help, and by golly, we're going to give it. A girl has gone missing."

"And her boyfriend!" Dooley piped up.

"And so we're going to search those woods. We're going to look under every branch, behind every tree, and under every rock until we've found them. And when we do, we can rest easy in the knowledge that we made a difference, and possibly saved a life. Or two," she added, with a nod in Dooley's direction.

I'd never heard anyone compare a missing person with a piece of kibble stuck behind a cupboard, or a buried bone, but her words didn't miss their effect. This group was fired up! And as they all cheered, she descended from her makeshift throne, looked on by stunned and mystified ladies and gentlemen, the regular visitors of the park, and we all moved out, singing a pleasant song as we did, with Harriet taking up the soprano part, as usual.

If Addie and Ted were in those woods, we'd find them—or die trying.

Okay, so maybe not. But we'd definitely give it our best shot!

CHAPTER 26

"What is that daughter of yours up to, I wonder?" said Vesta.

Tex, who'd been organizing his files—he still kept paper files on all of his patients, even though he probably should have digitized everything by now—looked up. "What do you mean?"

"Harriet told me this morning that Odelia is going to spend all day out in the woods. Said it had something to do with Edward Dexter."

"Oh, not again," said Tex. "I thought you said it was all over. That it was just a fling? A momentary weakness?"

"That's what I thought, especially when I saw Odelia and Chase so happy together last night. But now I'm not so sure." She gestured vaguely in the direction of the window. "You know that your daughter is out there right now? In those woods with Edward Dexter? And we all know what happens to innocent young girls when left alone in the woods with some horny old dude."

Tex swallowed. Simply picturing his one and only

daughter traipsing in those woods with her billionaire lover brought back images of red riding hood paying a visit to the big bad wolf. "He wouldn't..."

"Wouldn't what?"

"Take advantage of the situation, now would he?"

"Oh, wouldn't he? Show me a billionaire and I'll show you a guy whose hormone levels are off the charts. How else do you think they collect all those billions?"

"Through hard work and diligence?"

"Hormones, Tex! And now that man is focusing all of those hormones on your daughter!"

He gulped and almost dropped a file. "But what does he want from her?"

"What do all men want? Sex, of course, and plenty of it. Now what are you going to do about it is what I want to know?"

She had planted both hands on her sides and was eyeing him expectantly. He felt very strongly that he should do something, though he had no idea what. "What can I do?" he asked finally, when the solution escaped him.

"Go after them, of course! Save her from that man's horny hormones!"

"But I have a full roster of patients to see. I can't get away right now!"

"Oh, yes, you can. This is Odelia we're talking about, Tex. The mother of your granddaughter. The wife of your good friend Chase. And most importantly, the only daughter you'll ever have. So what are a few patients compared to saving the life of our most precious and beloved Odelia?"

"You're right," he said, galvanized by this pep talk. "And when you're right, you're right. We have to save her from herself and from that horrible man. And we have to do it now!" So he shoved the file folder back into position, and picked up his phone. "Cancel all my appointments," he told his loyal assistant-slash-receptionist-slash-mother-in-law. He'd always wanted to say that. It sounded so important.

"Now you're talking," Vesta grunted appreciatively. "Let's get out there and save a life, Doc Poole!"

CHAPTER 27

I don't know if you've ever searched a large swath of woods for a missing billionaire's daughter? If you have, you'll agree with me that it's not as easy as it sounds. These woods weren't made for walking, or at least big chunks of it weren't. Parts of it are a protected nature reserve, and as such can get a little impenetrable. Lucky for us, cats are small, and so we can reach into places where humans would have a hard time reaching. Like inside a hollowed-out tree, or in that genuine thicket created by a field of brambles.

And so it was that a couple of hours into our search for the missing couple, Dooley and I found ourselves entering a clearing, with a circle of mushrooms in the middle. It all looked a little like a fairy tale, and even featured a squirrel that was eyeing us suspiciously, probably wondering who these trespassers were.

"Hey there, squirrel," I said by way of greeting as we took a break by sitting down in the middle of the clearing. "Can I ask you a question, please, sir?"

"It's ma'am, not sir, and who are you anyway, and what are you doing in my home?"

"My name is Max, and this is Dooley," I said, gesturing to my friend, who'd closed his eyes and was about to take a refreshing nap. "We're looking for a missing couple. They were last seen two weeks ago, when their RV broke down on the side of the road. You wouldn't happen to have seen them, would you?"

"No, I would not," said the squirrel, softening now that she could see that we meant her no harm, and were merely passing through. "I don't usually see a lot of human activity in here, on account of the fact that humans aren't allowed to pass through this part of the woods."

"Yeah, I can see that," I said. "Well, that's too bad, cause the girl's dad is very worried, as you can probably imagine."

"Of course," said the squirrel, drawing closer and darting curious glances at Dooley. "Is he all right?"

"He's tired," I said. "We've been combing these woods for the past couple of hours, and it looks like it's going to be at least a couple of hours more."

The squirrel sat down at the edge of the circle of mushrooms, and said, "It's very nice of you to look for these people, Max. But if I were you I'd be careful."

"Careful? Why?"

"These woods aren't safe. There's a malevolent presence here that is very dangerous, at least if you're not used to living here, like I am."

"And what presence would that be?"

"I'm not sure, but it's not a laughing matter, this presence."

"But is it a person, or an animal?"

"Not an animal, and not really a person either," said the squirrel, musing for a moment. "I'd say it's something in between. Half man, half beast, if you will."

"And you've seen this man-beast?"

"Oh, sure. Many times. And I usually manage to steer clear of the thing. I can hear it coming, you see, and the moment it crosses my path, I simply skedaddle, hopping into the nearest tree and making sure not to be seen." She shivered freely, as if a sudden gust of icy wind had fluffed up her fur. "They say that one look from this evil presence can kill you stone-cold dead in your tracks. So whatever you do, never look into its eyes, Max."

"I won't," I promised the squirrel. I didn't want to tell her that I wasn't a firm believer in sorcery, or ghosts, or evil spirits, since she might take offense, but it did make me wonder if this man-beast, or whatever it was, might have something to do with the disappearance of Addie Dexter.

"Where does it live, this evil being?" I asked. "And how long has it been living in these woods?"

"It's been here since the dawn of time, or at least for as long as I can remember," said the squirrel, which wasn't saying much, since the average life span of a squirrel probably doesn't stretch as far back as the dawn of time.

"And where does it live?"

"Everywhere," said the squirrel. "I mean, it's an evil spirit, so it doesn't exactly need a particular place to live, you know. It can pop up anywhere, any time."

"So you've never seen a shack in these woods, or a cave or whatever?"

"It's an evil spirit, Max," said the squirrel emphatically. "It might very well be watching us right now, listening to every word we say. Or it might be miles away, hunting."

"It hunts, does it?"

"Of course it does."

"No, I mean, if it's a spirit being, it doesn't need to feed itself. Ghosts don't need their three square meals a day since they basically consist of vapor, I guess."

I have to confess I'm not really up to date on what makes a ghost or an evil spirit tick, but one thing I do know is that ghosts and spirits don't need sustenance, since they don't have a physical body, like you and I do.

"I can tell I'm dealing with a non-believer here," said the squirrel, getting up and dusting herself off. "So I'm only going to say this one last time, Max: watch your back, and if I were you, I'd get out of these woods, and don't come back."

And before I could ask a couple more questions—like: what was this ghost wearing, what did it look like, was it a man or a woman, that kind of stuff—the squirrel had scooted up a nearby tree and was gone.

And she hadn't even told us her name!

CHAPTER 28

"It has to be around here somewhere," said Vesta, parting some leafy branches.

"Are you sure?" asked Tex. "You said that five minutes ago already."

"The problem is that these trees all look the same," Vesta grumbled. "And not a single sign telling you where you're going. I'm telling you, Tex, there's a lot of room for improvement here. Something to take up with the town council."

"It's the woods, Vesta," said Tex. "There are never any signs in the woods."

"There should be. How else can anyone ever find their way in here?"

They'd been traipsing through these woods now for half an hour, and Tex had the distinct impression they were walking in circles. "I think we've seen that tree before," he now told his mother-in-law.

"What tree? What are you talking about?"

"That tree over there, with the gnarly branches. I'm sure we passed this tree before."

"All trees look the same, Tex," said Vesta. "I'm sure we're on the right track."

"How can you be so sure?"

"Women's intuition," she snapped.

"I don't like it here," said Scarlett, who'd also joined the search party. "It's creepy."

"It's not creepy, it's just dark and dank," Vesta said.

"Well, I think it's creepy, and I just broke a nail."

Scarlett, in spite of her friend's instructions, had refused to wear walking boots, and was dressed exactly the way she was always dressed: in high heels, short skirt and tank top. Though because she'd anticipated that temperatures in the woods might be outside of her comfort zone, she'd brought a sweater.

"As long as you don't break a leg," said Vesta, "you're fine."

"That nail cost me an arm and a leg," Scarlett complained. "And now it's gone. Just like that."

"You'll be gone just like that if you don't stop complaining and start cooperating," said Vesta.

"Ladies, ladies," said Tex. "Please let's not argue."

"I think it's ludicrous," said Scarlett, paying no attention to Tex. "Who told you that Odelia was meeting her lover for a secret tryst in the woods anyway? Wouldn't it be more convenient for them to meet at the Star Hotel, like regular people?"

"Odelia must have realized I was onto her," said Vesta. "So she decided to organize her next meeting in a place where no one would find her. But she didn't count on her dear old grandmother watching out for her." She swatted at a bug that had selected her neck as a landing strip. "Now if only we could find them."

"I'm starting to have second thoughts about this," said Scarlett. "I mean, so what if Odelia has an affair? What's so bad about that? People have affairs all the time. It's the most common thing in the world."

"Not my granddaughter," said Vesta.

"Not my daughter," said Tex.

"And besides, a billionaire is a great catch," said Scarlett. "I wish I could bag myself a billionaire," she added wistfully.

"Odelia has a perfectly good husband," said Vesta. "She doesn't need to fool around with any billionaires."

"Yeah, Chase is the best husband I could have wished for my girl," said Tex. And he wasn't lying. Like all fathers, he'd occasionally despaired for his daughter, when she brought yet another strange male specimen into their home, deposited it on their mat, and announced that this was to be her boyfriend from now on. Most of these boyfriends had gone out of their lives as quickly as they arrived, with a few exceptions, who'd hung on a little longer. But it wasn't until Chase had arrived on the scene that Tex had felt that now she had finally met the right one.

And then of course the long wait had begun, filled with even more tension and suspense: would it last? Would that headstrong daughter of theirs not turn her back on a good thing and dump this most promising son-in-law, like she had all the other, less worthy candidates to become Mr. Odelia Poole?

And just when life was smiling on them, and Odelia's future happiness seemed safe and secure, this Ed Dexter came along and threatened to ruin everything!

Unlike Vesta, he didn't think there was anything they could do about it. Odelia had never listened to her father's sage advice before, and she wasn't going to start now. But still. If there was a chance, no matter how small, that she could be convinced to listen to reason, they had to take it.

"Let's go home," Scarlett suggested. "If you can find our way home, that is."

"All you have to do is look on your phone and you'll know exactly where home is," said Vesta. And to show them how it was done, she took out her own phone and fired it up. "Huh," she said after a moment. "No reception. How about that?"

"No reception!" Scarlett cried, as if it was the worst fate that could have befallen her. "Are you kidding me?!"

"No, it says so right here. No reception." She shrugged. "I guess we'll just have to keep on walking, and put our faith in my women's intuition."

"Easy for you to say," Scarlett grumbled. "We'll never get out of these woods. We'll be walking around here forever, and when they find our bodies, about a year from now, they'll wonder why we were crazy enough to venture out here in the middle of nowhere in the first place!"

And they probably would have walked another couple of miles in circles, if not suddenly a familiar face appeared into view. It was Brutus, and the big black cat was accompanied by another familiar sight: Harriet!

"Oh, thank God," said Scarlett. "It's Harriet and Brutus! Quick, ask them where we are, Vesta."

And then Vesta did just that. A lot of meowing later, she translated the cats' words back to them. Basically it boiled down to: "We're also lost—and we were so glad to see you guys, hoping you could get us out of this mess!"

CHAPTER 29

Marge was seated on the porch swing, looking out across her domain, which was now a sort of devastated area. The snails were back in full force, and had by now eradicated what was left of the plants and flowers, and reduced Marge's precious little haven of green and peace into a wasteland.

"Such a shame," she said. "It was so nice and now look at it."

"What I don't understand is why these pests don't come into our garden," said Marcie, who was seated next to her on the swing. "Snails aren't usually this territorial, are they?"

"No, they're not." She'd done a little research and the websites all said that snails and slugs are attracted to leafy plants, moistness, rotting logs, paving stones under which they can hide, and generally a humid and shady area with plenty of food. But they could find that stuff in Marcie's backyard just as well, or Odelia's. So why did they favor hers?

"Maybe you should ask one of them experts," said Marcie as she took a sip from her cup of tea. "You know, a tree doctor or a botanist or whatever they're called. They might be able to tell you what's going on here."

"It's possible that we're growing a certain type of plant that they like," said Marge. "Or that our soil structure is different or something. Otherwise, I have no idea what's going on."

Both neighbors sat quietly for a moment, taking a nibble from the crispy ginger cookies Marcie had freshly baked, then Marcie piped up, "So what's going on with Odelia and her billionaire?"

"Oh, that's off," said Marge. "I think it was just one of those things. A fling, you know."

"I could have a fling with a billionaire," said Marcie with a light chuckle.

"Not me," said Marge. "I don't really care about that kind of stuff."

"Not that I'm not happy with Ted, mind you," Marcie was quick to say. "But a billionaire, Marge. It's the dream of every girl, isn't it?"

"Not me," Marge assured her neighbor. "Billionaires are people just like the rest of us, only richer, I guess."

"Yeah, a lot richer."

Marge had received a worrying message from Tex, but she didn't think it was a good idea to mention it to Marcie, who was a good neighbor and friend, but also one of the biggest blabbermouths in Hampton Cove, and that was saying something, for this town excelled in blabbermouths. Tex had written that he was going to the woods to catch Odelia and her billionaire in the act, and try and talk some sense into that daughter of theirs. Now what Odelia was doing in the woods with that billionaire fellow was beyond her. A picnic, maybe?

Just then, one of the snails that had taken over her garden came sliding up the swing. She eyed the creature with a touch of malevolence. She wasn't usually a bug hater, but when they came in like some invading army to destroy her precious plants and flowers, she could bear a grudge just as well as the next person.

So she took the snail between thumb and index finger, removed it from the swing, and lightly lobbed it back into the backyard, where it came from.

"And you say you removed all of them and they came back overnight?" asked Marcie.

"Yeah, we put them in Blake's field—as far away as possible, and this morning they were all back."

"So weird," said Marcie, shaking her head. She took another nibble from her cookie and another sip from her cup of tea. "Have you considered—"

"No, Marcie. We're not going to use poison."

"Oh, no. I wouldn't want you to, but there are other methods, you know."

"I know," she said. "But it's too late now anyway."

She just hoped the same wasn't true about Odelia.

※

"Do you believe in evil spirits, Max?" asked Dooley.

We'd put some distance between ourselves and that clearing, and had covered another big chunk of woods in the process. Still no sign of the evil spirit, though.

"No, I do not, Dooley," I said.

"But don't you think there's more under the sun than we know?"

"It's possible, but until I personally clap eyes on it, I'm skeptical about such phenomena."

"What about ghosts? Do you believe in ghosts?"

"No, I certainly don't," I said. "Ghosts are just a figment of an overactive imagination, Dooley. They don't exist."

"But what about the people who've seen a ghost? They can't all be lying, can they?"

"Have you ever met a person who saw a ghost?"

"No, but that doesn't mean they're not out there. The internet is full of stories of ghosts. And then there's the movies."

"Movies are fiction, Dooley. Anything is possible in a movie. And as far as the internet is concerned, we all know that anyone can say anything on there. So until I meet a ghost face to face, I like to remain skeptical if you don't mind."

"I'm also skeptical," said Dooley. "But I'm also a believer. I'm a skeptical believer, if you will."

And I'm sure he would have said a great deal more on the subject, if not suddenly we found ourselves entering yet another clearing. Only this clearing wasn't filled with a neat circle of mushrooms, but with a shack of some kind.

"Is that what I think it is, Max?" said Dooley, as we quickly hid behind a bush and hunkered down to study this strange phenomenon.

"Looks like someone is camping out here," I whispered.

"Could it be the evil spirit?"

"Evil spirits don't live in shacks, Dooley. Or roast things over an open fire," I added, pointing to the remnants of what must have been a nice fire, above which a stick had been placed, positioned on two more sticks, creating a sort of rotisserie.

Nothing stirred inside the shack, and for a moment I wondered if the person who'd stayed there had deserted it a long time ago. But then all of a sudden the door swung open, and a man emerged. He didn't look very clean, with smudges of dirt all over his face, his hair long and tangled, and a beard that looked like it might have been serving as a fly trap for the best part of the past couple of years.

"It's the evil spirit, Max!" said Dooley. "He's going to catch us!"

"You just might be right, Dooley," I said, studying the man. It wasn't Addie's boyfriend Ted, I thought. This guy looked at least sixty. But it was entirely possible this was the man that squirrel had been referring to. He looked a little ghostly, but only because he hadn't been taking good care of himself for a while.

"Let's get a little closer," I suggested, when the man slung a bag across his shoulder and set off into the woods, presumably to hunt for his next meal.

"Are you crazy! The spirit will catch us!"

"Nonsense," I said. "He's gone a-hunting, and he won't be back for a while. Let's go." And to set the example, I crept forward, and snuck in the direction of the shack. I wanted to take a look inside, and find out who this guy could possibly be.

Dooley reluctantly followed right behind me, and as we slipped into the shack, we found ourselves in a small space that can only be described as a bachelor's den, if said bachelor had been living rough for a number of years, and had been piling up junk in the meantime. I saw a small pile of books and magazines in the corner, a cot that had seen better days, but also different cell phones, a stack of cans, and some pots and pans and a washbasin, perhaps all pilfered from the cabins that dot these woods, and are rented out to the discerning tourist.

I couldn't find anything to ascertain the man's identity: no passport or names written down on a piece of paper.

"I don't think he's a ghost, Max," said Dooley after we'd been checking some of the guy's stuff. "Just a bum."

"A bum who's been out here for quite a while," I said as I

checked a copy of *Time Magazine* from ten years ago. "Okay, let's go. Nothing for us to see here."

I must admit I felt a little disappointed. This man obviously had no connection whatsoever with Addie Dexter. He was just a person who'd fallen through the cracks of society, and had made himself a new life out here as best as he could.

But just as we were about to slip back out, the door opened, and the man walked in!

We scuttled underneath the cot, and hoped he wouldn't take a seat or see us.

"Whatever happens, don't look into his eyes, Max!" said Dooley, clearly not having shaken his conviction that this man was an evil spirit.

And of course as luck would have it, the man did sit down on his cot!

"What is he doing?" I murmured as no sound reached our ears, and all we could see was the bottom of the man's very dirty pants and even dirtier old shoes.

Just then, his voice boomed through the small space.

"What do you want?" he growled, and I assumed he must have been speaking into one of those cell phones I'd seen lying around.

But how did he manage to recharge them if he didn't have any electricity?

"Just leave me alone," the man intoned. "No, I've got nothing more to say to you." He listened for a moment, and I could hear a person speak on the other side, but it was too faint to understand the words. "I don't care. Leave me alone!" And he must have disconnected, for he threw the phone on the floor, and got up.

For a few moments he paced up and down his shack, muttering strange oaths under his breath, then finally his feet moved out of view, and I had the impression he'd left again.

So poked my head from underneath that cot, even as Dooley said, "No, Max, wait!"

But too late.

A powerful hand grabbed me by the scruff of the neck, and I was lifted up into the air.

The man brought me face to face with him, and I couldn't help but look into his eyes. They were a clear blue, and somehow looked familiar. But I soon forgot about that, as he bared yellowed teeth, and said, "Looks like dinner is served!"

CHAPTER 30

"They say cat tastes like chicken," the man announced. "And I happen to like chicken."

"You're not really going to eat me, are you?" I said. "I'm not very nutritious. Too much flab, and we all know that flab isn't good for your cholesterol, not even when it's roasted over…" I gulped. "A slow fire!"

"You're a talkative fella, aren't you?" said the man. "Maybe I should wring your neck right now, just to shut you up!"

I got the message, and immediately lapsed into silence.

"Let him go, evil spirit!" suddenly a voice screamed.

It came from under the cot, and as even as I hissed, "Dooley, shut up!" Dooley wasn't deterred, but emerged from his hiding place, giving the man a kick against the leg.

"Let my friend go!" he repeated. But of course the man didn't understand what he was saying, and simply grabbed him by the neck and hoisted him up, effectively giving Dooley the same treatment he'd given me!

"Looks like it's my lucky day!" said the guy. "Two cats, if you please." He turned Dooley this way and that, and seemed disappointed with his catch. "Little skinny, aren't you? Lots of fur but no meat on those bones. Oh, well, beggars can't be choosers, I guess. And I'm not one to look a gift horse in the mouth."

"I'm not a horse! Let me go!" Dooley said, and tried to scratch the man's arm. Unfortunately it's very hard to really give of our best when they grab us by the neck like that. It's one of our weaknesses, but don't tell anyone I said that!

"Come on, Max, give this guy a punch in the snoot!" Dooley said.

"I would, if I could only reach his snoot!" I said.

"Feisty little creatures, aren't you," the man said with a wicked grin. "You'll pipe down soon enough. Now where am I going to keep you for the time being?"

"Unhand those cats, you brute!" suddenly a voice yelled.

We all turned—or at least the man turned, and as a consequence, so did we. And much to my surprise—and I imagine also to the bum—Gran was standing there, and behind her I could see Scarlett and Tex!

"Those are my cats," said Gran, "and if you don't put them down right this minute, I'll sue you for damaging my personal property!"

"I'd set them down if I were you, buddy," said Tex, as he stepped into the shack. "She's very cranky, on account of the fact that we've been walking for hours, and our feet hurt."

"And we still haven't found Odelia and her secret lover," Scarlett grumbled, also joining us. Immediately, and without waiting for a personal invitation, she sank down on the cot and started massaging her painful feet.

"What is this?" said the man, shocked and dismayed. "Get out of here right now!"

"Oh, simmer down," said Gran. "You haven't by any chance seen a blond-haired woman with a billionaire, have you?"

"Who are you people?" the man demanded.

PURRFECT SLUG

"My name is Tex Poole," said Tex, introducing himself and holding out a hand.

"Very clever tactic," I told Dooley. "Now he'll be forced to put us down."

Only the guy clearly hadn't a polite bone in his body, for he blithely ignored Tex's hand, and held onto to us instead.

"I'm a doctor," Tex clarified, retracting the fin. "And this is my mother-in-law Vesta Muffin, and her friend, Scarlett Canyon."

A normal person would have given his own name at this point, but this guy clearly wasn't normal, for he said, "If you don't get out of here right now..."

"Can you put those cats down already?" said Gran. "I mean, I've told you once, I've told you twice, and now I'm telling you a third time, and you're still holding onto them."

"Yeah, put us down," I said. "I'm getting a pain in the neck."

And he must have understood, for he did set us down.

"Finally!" said Dooley. "And now let's attack, Max!"

"Let's not," I said, putting a paw on my painful neck and massaging it gently.

"You wouldn't happen to have a cream for swollen feet, would you?" asked Scarlett. "Only I didn't bring my walking shoes."

"I told you to bring them," said Gran. "But you wouldn't listen, as usual."

"Nice place you got here," said Tex conversationally, as he inspected the stack of magazines. "And I like what you've done with… the decorations."

"Can you just clear off!" said the man, still not falling into his role as the welcoming host.

"In a minute," said Scarlett. "When I can walk again."

"What were you doing with my cats, anyway?" asked Gran.

"We were hiding under his cot when he found us," I explained.

"We thought he was an evil spirit, because the squirrel said so," said Dooley. "But Max says evil spirits don't exist, and he's just an old bum."

"So what's your name, buddy?" asked Gran.

"Cyril Wellbeloved," said Tex, having leafed to the first page of a book he'd picked up. "Have we met before, Cyril?"

"My name isn't Cyril," said the man gruffly. "And besides, what's it to you?"

"Like I said, I'm a doctor," said Tex, "and that welt you've got on your hand looks pretty painful. I could look at that for you if you want."

The guy stared down at his hand, as if realizing for the first time that he had one, and in one fluid movement held it under Tex's nose. The doctor frowned at the appendage, took careful hold of it, and examined the welt, which did indeed look pretty red and swollen.

"So what happened here, Cyril, if I may ask?"

"You may not," Cyril growled unhappily.

"I'd say this is infected, Cyril," said Tex finally. "Can you come into my office first thing tomorrow morning? We'll clean this wound, and bandage this up nice and proper." He patted the man's shoulder. "Should be back in working order in no time. Now if you could show us the way back to town, I'd be much obliged."

"We're not going back until we've found Odelia and this Dexter fellow and have broken up their tryst," said Gran stubbornly.

At the mention of the name Dexter, Cyril seemed to stiffen for a moment, but then he shook it off.

"If you head straight that way," he said, "you'll reach the road in about half an hour. Turn left, and follow the road and it will take you into Hampton Cove."

"Gee, that's so nice of you, Cyril," said Tex, giving the man's shoulder a squeeze. "And don't forget to come into my office tomorrow? If that hand doesn't get treated, it might get worse, and the infection might spread. And once that happens, you're a lot worse off, I can tell you that much," he concluded cheerfully.

"Tex has a great cotside manner, doesn't he, Max?" said Dooley.

"He really has," I said. "Though it seems to have the opposite effect on Cyril."

"For the last time, my name isn't Cyril!" said Cyril. "And now clear out, all of you, and take those damn cats with you!"

I didn't need to be told twice, and was out of there like a shot. Gran was right behind me, and so was Tex. Scarlett took some more convincing, but finally she joined us, hobbling a little, and we were on our way in the direction indicated.

"Do cats really taste like chicken, Max?" asked Dooley.

"I don't know, Dooley," I said. "I've never eaten a cat. And I hope I never will."

He shivered. "Good thing Gran came when she did. We would have been dinner otherwise!"

"So what were you doing out there, Gran?" I asked, hurrying to keep up with the humans, who were setting a brisk pace.

"Looking for Odelia and Edward Dexter," Gran said. "She and that Dexter guy are having an affair, and if it's the last thing I do, I'm going to make it stop."

"But she's not having an affair," I said. "I already told Harriet last night. She's just helping him find his daughter."

"A likely story," Gran scoffed. "No, she's having an affair, all right. I saw them with my own two eyes. And so did you, isn't that right, Scarlett?"

"My feet hurt!" Scarlett cried. "Why didn't you tell me we were going hiking?"

"I did tell you, you silly woman."

"No, you didn't. You said we were going to catch Odelia and Dexter in the act. Nothing about hiking in some stupid woods."

"Relax. We're almost at that road."

"Nice fellow, this Cyril Wellbeloved," said Tex conversationally. "Though what he's doing out here is beyond me. Not very pleasant, especially in winter."

"Do you know this guy, Gran?" I asked.

"Nope. Never seen him before in my life. You, Tex? This guy familiar to you?"

"I can't say that he is," said Tex. "Though his name does sound familiar somehow." He shook his head. "It'll come to me. It always does. And usually in the middle of the night when I have to get up and go to the bathroom."

I wasn't particularly interested in Tex's bathroom habits, and neither, it seemed, were Gran or Scarlett. The latter was only interested in that road.

"High heels aren't fit for hiking, are they, Max?" asked Dooley, as he studied Scarlett's painful gait.

"No, they certainly are not."

We'd had a lucky escape, but all I could think was that I'd seen that man before somewhere, and if the name Cyril Wellbeloved sounded familiar to Tex, the answer of the riddle was hopefully forthcoming. Now all we had to do was wait until he had to get up in the middle of the night to go to the bathroom.

CHAPTER 31

Cyril Wellbeloved—or not-Cyril Wellbeloved, as he insisted—stared after the departing trio with the two cats, and spat on the ground. It was a shame he'd have to forego a nice meal, but at least he was rid of these intruders. In all the years he'd been living in the woods, never had anyone interrupted his peace and quiet like this. Oh, he'd had visitors, of course, but not like these three, who thought they could just come in and boss him around. Especially that old woman was the worst. Who did she think she was, telling him what to do in his own home?

He spat on the ground again for good measure, and walked to the edge of the clearing, glanced left and right, just to make sure those nosy parkers were well out of earshot, and knocked three times on the protruding piece of metal at his feet. If you didn't know it was there, you'd never find it, which was the whole idea.

From inside the enclosure, a hollow voice said, "Are they gone?"

"Yeah, they're gone," he said. "You can come out now."

"Good," said the voice. "I thought they'd never leave."

Our first day of searching was at an end, and we didn't have much to show for our effort. We all met back where we'd set out, and reported to Odelia, who'd also returned from her search, along with Chase.

Neither had found anything of note, and when one by one the teams of cats dropped by, they all had the same message: no sign of the missing couple. And apart from Cyril, no sign of life in general, or at least human life.

"We saw a ghost," Dooley announced. "He almost ate us, but Gran saved us."

Gran regarded Odelia with a critical eye. "We need to have a word, young lady," she said.

"Later, Gran. I have to finish welcoming our teams back."

"Tonight. And don't think you can get out of this by postponing," she warned. "I know what you did," she added, wagging her finger. "And I won't stand for it!"

Odelia frowned at her grandmother, but the old lady had already turned on her heel and was walking away.

"What was that all about?" asked Odelia, puzzled.

Her dad, who stood rocking back and forth on his heels, gave a weak smile. "Oh, you know your grandmother," he said. Never a man keen on confrontation, he didn't seem about to get involved in one now. And since Chase was present, he wasn't going to bring up the tryst business.

"I'm actually hoping the dogs might have sniffed out some kind of clue," Odelia confessed, as she tapped an impatient pencil on her notepad.

"I'll have you know that cats are better at tracking people than dogs," said Harriet, who'd overheard this last snippet of conversation. "In fact cats' sense of smell is practically on par with dogs, if not better."

"It's more complicated than you think, Harriet," said

Dooley. "I saw a documentary on the Discovery Channel last week, and some dog breeds have more scent receptors than cats. About a hundred million more, in fact."

"Oh, who cares," said Harriet. "That's probably fake news anyway."

"On the other hand, cats have more V1R receptors, which are instrumental in differentiating between different scents, so they have a more sensitive nose."

"Go away, Dooley."

"So on the whole cats do have a better sense of smell than dogs," Dooley concluded.

Harriet perked up at this. "Now you're talking."

"Though the best noses belong to rats. They beat cats and dogs paws down."

"There are the dogs now," I said. "Let's see what they found."

Fifi and Rufus came trudging up, followed by a small contingent of about fifteen canines.

"Nothing," Fifi said the moment she arrived in our midst. I dutifully translated her message for Odelia, whose face sagged.

"Not a single clue?" I asked.

"Nope. If this Addie person was ever in these woods, I didn't pick up anything."

Edward Dexter had, on Odelia's instigation, handed her a T-shirt that belonged to his daughter, and Odelia had held it out for the dogs to sniff, preparatory to their excursion.

"I didn't get nothing either," said Rufus. "And now we missed a whole day of training for our show." He didn't look happy, and neither did Fifi, though the latter wasn't overly concerned about the show, it seemed. And as she drew me aside, she explained why this was.

"I've decided not to take part in the show," she said.

"But why?" I said. "I thought you were so excited?"

"I was, until I saw one of those shows on TV. It's just a bunch of show dogs, isn't it?"

"Well, yes," I said. "That's the whole point."

"I don't want to be a show dog. Being primped and prepped, and having to jump through hoops like a moron? No, thank you very much. It's just so degrading, Max. As if all we're good for is to look pretty in front of a crowd. Now if they'd ask me about the books I like to read, or the songs I like to sing, or even my political views or my personal philosophy. But no, it's all about good looks. Yuck."

She returned to the rest of the pack, who were delivering their progress report to Harriet, who dutifully translated everything to Odelia. It soon became clear that there actually wasn't all that much to report. And so the briefing was over very quickly, and then it was time to head on out and return home.

As Dooley and I rode in the car with Odelia and Chase, and so did Harriet and Brutus, along with Fifi and Rufus, we talked about the bum we'd caught in the woods, and how we'd almost ended up in his pot. And as Dooley related the story in vivid detail, I couldn't shake the feeling this meeting meant something.

But what? And why?

CHAPTER 32

"I'm worried, Scarlett," said Vesta as they traveled back in her car—or rather her daughter's car, which she had more or less confiscated. "And I'm troubled."

"Me, too," Scarlett said as she checked her feet. She turned to Tex, who was riding in the back. "Can you give me something for these, Tex, sweetie? I'm not sure I'll ever be able to walk again."

"I'll take a look at them later, if you want," said Tex, who seemed a million miles away.

"My mind is not at ease," Vesta continued what practically amounted to a monologue, since Scarlett was only concerned with her painful feet, and Tex might just as well have been on a different planet for all the attention he paid her. "Odelia acted as if she didn't know what I was talking about, but I'm not fooled. No, sir, I am not."

"Did you just call me sir?" asked Scarlett as she massaged her feet.

And then it hit her. "You know what we should do? Go straight to the source! Yes, sir!"

"Again with the sir," said Scarlett. "And what source are you talking about?"

"The source of trouble, of course. Clearly Odelia has been seduced by this billionaire, and so he can just as easily disseduce her, or is it unseduce?"

"Neither, I would say," said Scarlett.

"What do you think, Tex?" asked Vesta.

Tex once again emerged as if from a dream. "Mh?" he said.

"I said we should go straight to the source of the problem. Root it out."

"Excellent idea," said Tex. "Chop off their heads, you think? Smush them?"

"I wish," said Vesta. "But Alec wouldn't take kindly to his mother chopping off the head of a billionaire. No, we just have to find something we can hold over the guy."

"Blackmail, you mean?" asked Scarlett, who'd fished a toffee from the glove compartment and was sucking on it with visible delight.

"I wouldn't call it blackmail, exactly. So what do we have on the guy?"

"Nothing," said Scarlett. "As far as I can tell, Edward Dexter is squeaky clean."

"Wasn't there a scandal of some kind? Something about insider trading?"

"I wouldn't go there, if I were you, Vesta," said Scarlett. I don't even understand what that is all about, much less use it to make the guy break up with Odelia."

Tex once more emerged as if from a trance, shaking his head like a dog. "Wait, what? Who's breaking up with Odelia?"

"Oh, do pay attention, Tex," said Vesta. "We're trying to find something we can use to make Dexter break up with Odelia. Only we don't know him well enough."

PURRFECT SLUG

"No, I guess we don't," said Tex, and once more returned to la-la land.

"Which is why we need to do some digging," said Vesta, following her train of thought to its logical conclusion. "Which means..." And then she got one of those brainwaves you always read so much about, but which so rarely happen to ordinary folk like her. "I've got it!" she shouted, causing Tex almost to hit the ceiling, and Scarlett to give her frowny looks.

"Will you please keep your eyes on the road?" said her friend. "If you keep this up we'll end up in a ditch."

"All we have to do is find something incriminating. Doesn't matter what. Anything that this Dexter fellow doesn't want the world to know."

"I think we already established that we don't know him well enough to have that kind of dirt on him."

"No, but we know where to find it, don't we?"

"We do?"

"Of course! Where do people keep the stuff they don't want anyone to know about?"

"Um... buried in the backyard?"

"Oh, please cooperate, Scarlett," said Vesta, "and use that brain of yours."

"I am using my brain. Only it's very hard to focus when your feet are killing you."

"In his safe, that's where. So we break into his house, burgle his safe, find something incriminating, and then we pay him a visit, promising not to tell anyone about what we found, on the condition that he never darken our doorstep again." She beamed at her friend, who immediately grabbed the wheel and yanked it to the right.

"Phew," said Scarlett. "Almost one less cyclist in the world. And what was all that about burgling a safe?"

"You and I are going to break into Edward Dexter's house

tonight. We find what we need and get out again. Easy peasy!"

"Easy peasy, my ass. I've never burgled a safe in my life, and I'll bet this guy has a world-class alarm system."

"Yeah, I guess so," she said, not having foreseen this snag. Alarm systems were a nuisance. Unless... She glanced in the rearview mirror at her son-in-law, who once again had disappeared in his own mind, such as it was.

"Tex!"

Tex jumped. "Eh?"

"I have a very important assignment for you."

"You have?"

"Yes, so listen very carefully. I want you and Marge to pay a visit to Edward Dexter tonight."

"Dexter? Who's Dexter?"

"Your daughter's secret lover, and possibly your future son-in-law if we don't put a stop to this nonsense right speedily!"

Tex grimaced. "I'd totally forgotten about Dexter."

"So you and Marge pay a visit to Dexter tonight. You tell him that you want to meet your daughter's new boyfriend."

"I can't tell him that!" said Tex.

"Okay, so then invent some other story. The important thing is that you leave the front door open, so Scarlett and I can easily walk in. And while you keep the guy occupied in the living room, or one of his rooms at any rate, we'll go and look for his safe, and burgle it!"

"You still haven't told me how we're going to get into the guy's safe," said Scarlett, as she had transferred her attention from her painful feet to the fingernail that had gone AWOL.

"Oh, don't worry about that. We'll figure it out as we go along. I mean, how hard can it be, right?" When Scarlett gave her a look of utter incredulity, she said, "We'll google it! YouTube is probably full of videos on how to burgle a safe."

"Oh, sure. We'll watch a YouTube video while we break into the safe of one of the richest men on the planet. Easy peasy."

"Sarcasm," said Vesta. "Not a good look, Scarlett."

"I don't care how it looks. I don't want to end up in jail again."

"We're the neighborhood watch. If Dexter catches us we'll simply tell him that we're doing a stress test of his alarm system."

"A stress test. Really?"

"Trust me, he'll be thrilled. Billionaires love that kind of stuff. He'll probably pay us handsomely for the privilege, especially when we actually manage to break into his safe, and prove to him how fallible his security is."

"If you say so," said Scarlett dubiously.

"So what do you say, Tex?" asked Vesta, directing a questioning look at her son-in-law. "Tex!"

Once more, Tex jumped to attention. "Eh? What?"

"You and Marge. Tonight. Edward Dexter. Got it?" When the good doctor hesitated a little too long in her view, she added, "Or do you want Grace to grow up without a father?"

"Okay, fine," said Tex. "I'll do it. But when you get caught, I'm denying all knowledge."

"We won't get caught."

"In fact I'll deny knowing you."

"Oh, Tex, you break my heart," said Scarlett with a slight grin in Vesta's direction.

"We won't get caught," Vesta repeated, gripping the steering wheel a little tighter, and almost mowing a pedestrian off the sidewalk. She was a woman on a mission. A mission to save her granddaughter's life. And she was not going to fail. No, sir!

CHAPTER 33

I had actually been hoping for a quiet night in, after the eventful day we'd had, but I probably should have known this wasn't going to be in the cards. Being a member of the Poole family and quiet nights at home don't go together, I'm afraid.

The first thing we discovered was that the snails, having exhausted their supply of fresh greens, had decided to look at yonder shores for their vitaminary and nutritious needs, and had launched a two-pronged attack: one contingent had dispatched to Odelia and Chase's backyard, and a second, possibly even larger battalion had moved into Ted and Marcie's. And so when we burst onto the scene, Harrington Street was up in arms.

Ted and Marcie, who'd hitherto expressed quiet sympathy, now threw angry glances at Tex, whom they blamed for this predicament, and tried to salvage what they could from the slaughter. While Odelia and Chase, having arrived home after a disappointing mission, and had also hoped to settle down for a little while to think and regroup, saw their precious floral delight being reduced to nothingness by a horde of ravenous slugs and snails.

"What do we do!" Tex was yelling.

"We do what we did last night," said Chase, taking control of the situation, like the stalwart keeper of the peace that he was: "We apprehend and neutralize."

"You mean, we kill them?" Tex cried, grabbing at his hair. "But I can't, Chase. As much as I would like to, I can't. I'm a doctor. I save lives, not take them!"

"We don't use lethal force, we merely extract," Chase said in that calm way of his. "We grab the slugs, deposit them into these plastic receptacles, and this time we take them much further afield. In fact we take them as far as—"

"Don't say the park, Chase," said Marge. "We can't destroy the park, just to save our own backyard."

"I was going to say the woods," said Chase. "But the park is probably a better idea. It's big enough, Marge," he assured the stricken woman. "They can't possibly eat the entire park. There's not enough of them. And besides, in the park they'll meet natural predators, who will cut down their number to a manageable size."

"Are you sure?"

"Trust me," said Chase, and placed a reassuring arm around his mother-in-law's shoulder.

For some reason this gesture opened the floodgates, and soon Marge was crying her heart out, and pressing her face into Chase's broad chest.

"Looks like this snail business really got to her," said Dooley.

"It's not the snail business," I said. "It's the Odelia and Dexter business."

"What business?"

"Never mind," I said. "Let's get out of their way before they pick us up and deposit us in the park, too."

"I wouldn't mind being deposited in the park," said Brutus. "It's probably a lot more peaceful there than it is here."

Just then, Harriet came hurrying up. "Tragedy struck!" she cried.

"Now what?" I said.

"Fifi says she's not going to compete, and neither is Rufus! All of my work down the drain—just like that!"

"But why?" asked Brutus.

"She says being in a show is degrading. It's beneath her. She wants to be praised for her intellect, not her good looks. Oh, how ungrateful. After all I've done for those two."

"Poor Harriet," said Dooley once Harriet was out of earshot.

"Yeah, poor Harriet," I said with a smile. "It's a real tragedy."

We moved into the house, and let the humans engage in another evening spent catching snails. It's a pastime not often practiced in these parts, but it's good clean family fun, and I can recommend it to anyone. Even kids can join in, as evidenced by Grace, who tried to put a snail into her mouth, but was caught just in time by Odelia's uncle Alec.

And as I settled down on the couch, after having eaten my fill, and was ready for a prolonged nap, Gran came in, and took a seat next to us on that same couch.

I'd fully expected her to turn on the TV and catch some of her favorite shows, but instead she lowered her voice and said, "I need you guys for a secret mission."

I yawned. "What mission?" I asked, in spite of myself and my reluctance to engage in any more missions for one day.

"We're going to collect some dirt on this Dexter guy, so we can make him give up Odelia," she said with a satisfied smile. "And I need you to come along to be our eyes and ears. Just in case he's got his security people traipsing around.

Those billionaires always got security," she added with a touch of rancor at those naughty billionaires who tried to protect their wealth from thieves and burglars.

"Why would you want to do that, Gran?" asked Dooley.

"Isn't it obvious? Odelia is having an affair with the guy, and we need some leverage to make him give her up. We've got a marriage to save, Dooley. So are you in or out?"

"But... I thought that was just a figment of your imagination?" said Dooley, cutting me a curious glance.

"Imagination, my foot," said Gran. "I know what I saw, and that was no innocent hug, like you guys claim it was. I know pure savage lust when I see it, and that guy's got sex on the brain. Now are you prepared to do what needs to be done to save my poor innocent granddaughter? Or are you too chicken?"

At the mention of the word chicken, Dooley shivered. "Please don't talk about chicken, Gran," he lamented. "It brings back memories."

"Okay, fine. I'm sorry. I shouldn't have said that. But are you coming or not? Cause I'm planning this whole operation, and I need to know if I should engage Harriet and Brutus, or if I can count on you two."

"You can count on us," I said immediately. "We're going to help you dig up dirt on that billionaire, and save Odelia from his clutches."

"Now you're talking," said Gran, well pleased as she patted me on the head. "I knew you'd see the light." She got up. "I'll pick you guys up at eight o'clock sharp. Wait for me in front of the house. And whatever happens, don't tell Odelia!"

"We won't," I promised her.

Once she was gone, Dooley was staring at me with a look of astonishment on his furry face. "I don't understand, Max. I thought you said the whole thing was a big misunderstanding? That Odelia and Dexter aren't having an affair?"

"They are not," I assured my friend. "But I've always wanted to see what a billionaire's home looks like, and how often do you get an opportunity like this?"

"Not often," he admitted. "Still, it's probably illegal what Gran is planning."

"Oh, it's extremely illegal. But that doesn't mean it can't also be a lot of fun."

"Fun," said Dooley unhappily. "Fun is having a nice nap on the couch. Fun is having a great night at cat choir. Fun isn't being caught by a cat-eating maniac, or breaking into people's homes." He sighed. "I just hope this guy doesn't think cats taste like chicken, too."

CHAPTER 34

I have to say I wasn't all that keen on accompanying Gran on this excursion. She has a tendency of overdoing things and letting her zeal get her into trouble. Then again, Marge and Tex had also signed off on the plan, so perhaps it wasn't as crazy a scheme as I thought it was.

And so the evening's entertainment began. Marge and Tex were the first to leave, as they had to act as the distraction that would enable the rest of us to sneak in and do our business.

We rode with Gran and Scarlett, and as we approached the house, the old lady parked across the street, keeping a close eye on the Pooles, who at that moment had already gotten out of their car and were walking up to the house.

"This is it, you guys," said Gran excitedly. "It's happening!"

And it was. Tex applied his finger to the doorbell of what was arguably an impressive house, though not as impressive as some of the mansions I'd seen.

"It's not as big as I thought it would be," said Scarlett.

"No, it's definitely not as big as Charlie Dieber's house," said Gran. "Or Donna Bruce's old place."

"Maybe he doesn't like big houses?" Scarlett suggested.

"Or maybe he's stingy," Dooley suggested. "And that's why his daughter ran off with her boyfriend to join the circus. Because he wouldn't fund her lavish lifestyle, and allow her to live in the lap of luxury."

"Let's just wait and see what it looks like inside," I suggested. "These places always look much bigger on the inside than the outside suggests."

"Of course," said Gran. "These billionaires try to be discreet and not attract too much unwanted attention."

Whatever the case, Marge and Tex had been allowed into the house, and as they entered, Marge half turned and gave us a look of significance.

"And we're on," said Gran.

We got out of the car as quickly as possible, and moved up to the house.

"Looks like Marge managed to do as I asked," Gran whispered, as she gently pushed against the door, which yielded to the pressure and easily swung open.

"Are you sure about this, Vesta?" asked Scarlett, experiencing those last-minute jitters.

"Yes, I'm sure," Gran snapped, and without further ado entered the house.

We all followed in her footsteps, and when she told us to spread out and meet her back there in ten minutes, we didn't waste any time, and did as we were told.

"I just hope he doesn't have dogs," Dooley intimated. "I like dogs, but not all dogs like cats."

Gran and Scarlett disappeared upstairs, and Dooley and I decided to investigate the ground floor.

I could hear voices coming from somewhere nearby. Undoubtedly Marge and Tex were getting better acquainted with our Mr. Dexter.

"What are we looking for, exactly, Max?" asked Dooley.

PURRFECT SLUG

"No idea. Anything that strikes us as interesting, I guess."

"Gran wants us to find something increaminating," said Dooley. "So maybe we should check the kitchen. Most humans keep their cream in the fridge."

"I don't think she was referring to cream," I said. "She wants something she can use to blackmail the guy."

"Why does Gran want to blackmail Mr. Dexter?"

"Because she believes he's having an affair with Odelia, which he's not."

"It's all getting very complicated, isn't it, Max?" Dooley lamented.

We'd arrived at what looked like a study of some kind, with plenty of bookcases lining the walls, and a large desk with a laptop computer, that was humming pleasantly in the background.

"Oh, look," said Dooley. "Mr. Dexter's computer. Maybe it's mining shitcoins."

"Bitcoins, Dooley, not shitcoins," I corrected my friend. "And I don't think that's what this laptop is doing. To mine bitcoin you need a much bigger computer."

Still, my interest was attracted by that laptop. I just hoped it wasn't protected with a password. It's a very annoying habit humans have to protect everything with a password.

So I hopped onto the office chair neatly placed in front of that desk, and tapped the spacebar of the laptop with my paw. Immediately the computer sprang to life, showing a picture of a very large and very orange cat. I stared at the cat for a moment, wondering why Mr. Dexter would have put my image up on his computer as a screensaver, but then I realized this wasn't me but some other orange cat. I just hoped this particular specimen wasn't anywhere in the vicinity, for it looked huge!

As it was, though, the laptop was locked, as I had expected, and needed Mr. Dexter's finger to unlock it. And since I didn't have that particular finger at my immediate disposal, I heaved a sigh of disappointment and hopped down again from my perch.

And that's when it happened: there was a loud snarl, a sort of whizzing motion, and suddenly our exit was blocked by a very large, very orange cat!

"Gotcha!" this cat announced, displaying a vicious sort of grimace as it uttered these fateful words.

"Oh, hey, there," I said, trying to keep my cool, though inside I wasn't feeling at all sanguine about this fateful meeting. If this cat started meowing and alerting its master, we were definitely in a pickle.

"My name is Max," I said, by way of introduction, "and this is Dooley."

The cat stared from me to Dooley and back again, and broke into a sort of wide grin. "Max! Of course! We've met before, remember? At cat choir? I was supposed to sing with the basses but Shanille told me my pitch was too high, so she put me with the tenors instead, and I ended up standing next to you. You were even kind enough to show me the ropes."

"That's right!" I said. "Now I remember. You have a very nice singing voice... um..."

"Dex Dexter," said the cat, and held up his right paw. "Put it there, brother."

And so I put it there, and so did Dooley, though the latter did so with a touch of trepidation. Dex was a big cat, easily twice my size, and I'm not a kitten myself.

"So Mr. Dexter is your human," I said. "I didn't know."

"Oh, it's a long story," said Dex. "He wasn't always my human, you know. But I won't bore you with the details. So how have you guys been? It's been too long since I managed to squeeze cat choir into my schedule. Busy busy, you know."

"Yeah, I know," I said, though I didn't. Then again, these

billionaires probably jet around the world on a continuous basis. Tokyo today, St Barts tomorrow.

"We're looking for something incriminating on your human," said Dooley, who hadn't forgotten our mission. "So that we can make him break up his non-existing relationship with our human. It's all very complicated," he admitted. "I don't understand it myself."

"Your human and my human? Hey, what a blast," said Dex. "That means we're going to be housemates from now on. How about that?"

"I don't think so," I said. "Mr. Dexter hired Odelia to find his daughter for him, and now Odelia's grandmother thinks they're having an affair, just because Odelia gave Mr. Dexter a hug. It's all one big misunderstanding," I explained.

"I'll bet it is," said Dex, looking puzzled all of a sudden. "Cause as far as I know, my human doesn't have a daughter."

CHAPTER 35

"What do you mean, he doesn't have a daughter?" I asked.

"It's part of that long and complicated story I didn't want to bore you with," said Dex as he took a seat. "But if you insist, I might be persuaded to tell you all about it. But not now, and not here. Frankly I've been hoping to join cat choir again, and now with you guys showing up, I'm thinking this must be some kind of sign."

"It might be," I said carefully. I'm not big on signs, but if Dex thought our arrival on his doorstep was one, and it induced him to tell us the story of his life, I was all for it.

"Okay, so let's get out of here, and I'll tell you all about it on the way. How does that sound?"

"But we haven't even found anything incriminating yet," said Dooley.

"I think we owe it to Dex to take him to cat choir, don't you?" I said, giving my friend a knowing wink, which I hoped he'd catch.

He didn't, but still stopped harping on the incriminating part of our mission, and tagged along.

"Let's head out the back door," Dex suggested. And as we did, I caught a whiff of some powerful and faintly familiar scent. It was a yeasty odor of some kind, and when I asked Dex about it, he explained that Mr. Dexter's gardener had complained about snails and slugs infesting his precious garden, and had been trying a true and tried technique to get rid of them.

"Our human's backyard is also having a snail problem," Dooley confessed. "And their solution is to catch the snails one by one and deposit them elsewhere."

"Don't get me wrong, snails are a very useful and beneficial species," said Dex, who had perked up a great deal as we went on our way. He clearly wasn't a homebody, and enjoyed being out and about. "They're very beneficial for getting rid of rotten leaves, or anything decaying, and also they spread some very useful nutrients and manure in your backyard, which feeds the plants. The only problem is when you have too many of them, and they start eating your regular plants and flowers, which they rarely do, mostly focusing on the rotting stuff."

"Exactly the problem we have!" said Dooley. "There's simply too many of them, and they've turned Tex and Marge's backyard, and now also Odelia's, into a wasteland."

"Okay, so what's the story with Edward Dexter and his daughter?" I said. All this talk about snails was all well and good, but what I really wanted to know was the Dexter business.

"Remember how I told you that Mr. Dexter wasn't always my human? Well, that's because I used to belong to his brother Edward."

"But… this guy is Edward, isn't he?"

"No, the Mr. Dexter you know is actually Andrew, Edward's twin brother."

"Huh." Now this was news.

"So I used to belong to Edward. Only he went through some sort of breakdown, and had to step down from his position at the head of his company, and asked his brother to take his place. Just for the time being, you know. Until he got back on his feet. But it's been ten years now, and we still haven't heard from Edward. So obviously I'm worried that something might have happened to him, and that he might never come back." He shrugged. "Though Andrew treats me well enough, I guess. He's not a cat person, per se, but he tries hard to be."

"So... the guy who lives in that house isn't Edward?" I asked, just to be clear.

"Nope. Andrew stepped in as chairman of the board and CEO or whatever, and he also moved into the house. Before this happened he ran a fishing tackle store in Boca Raton. He had to learn on the job, but I think he's done a pretty good job. And of course he's got plenty of talented folk actually running the company."

"But... so who's Addie?"

"Addie is Edward's daughter."

"And she's also been living with Andrew?"

Dex nodded. "She was still very young at the time, of course. A teenager. So the transition happened more or less smoothly. But yeah, Andrew is her uncle, not her dad."

"Okay," I said, thinking hard.

"It's very kind of Andrew to take over for his brother like that," said Dooley. "It shows his good heart."

"Yeah, he's all right," said Dex. "And of course we're not dogs, so we don't form this silly attachment to our humans dogs suffer from." He laughed, but I could tell that his heart wasn't in it.

"You miss Edward, don't you?" I said.

He nodded, and his eyes grew moist. It told me that he

might not be a dog, but he'd much rather have Edward back, no matter how hard Andrew tried to be a good pet parent.

"Okay, so this throws a different light on this matter altogether," I said. "It's entirely possible that the reason Addie went missing has something to do with this whole twin brother thing."

"Addie didn't go missing," said Dex with a frown. "Who told you that?"

"Why, Edward—um, Andrew, of course. It's why Odelia got involved. He asked her to track down his daughter, since the authorities couldn't."

Dex burst out laughing. "Max, he's pulling your leg! Addie isn't missing. She's off on a road trip with her boyfriend Ted. Probably having the time of their lives."

Obviously Dex wasn't as well informed as he thought he was, and since I didn't want him to worry, I decided not to mention the fact that Addie hadn't returned from her road trip.

"So how well does Addie get along with her uncle?" I asked instead.

"Well, obviously they don't have the kind of relationship a father and daughter would have, but they get along great. Addie adores her uncle, and he's crazy about his niece, probably feeling sorry for the way her dad abandoned her."

"They don't know where Edward is?"

"Not a clue. The guy just went up in smoke one day."

"Odd. You'd think a big CEO like that would stay in touch."

"Yeah, you would think so. But you'd be wrong."

I noticed a touch of bitterness in the orange cat's voice, and I didn't wonder. "So is he married, this Andrew?"

"Nope. Never found the one. At least not yet."

"He's finally found the one in Odelia," said Dooley. "She'll be like a mother to Addie, and it's so great that Grace will have a big sister now." Then he seemed to realize what he was saying, for he turned to me. "Oh, no, Max! We have to find Addie, or else Grace will grow up without a sister!"

I sighed. "Oh, Dooley."

CHAPTER 36

"Who would have thought, right?" said Dooley.
"Mh," I said.
"Edward isn't Edward but Andrew. And he's not Addie's dad but her uncle."
"Mh."
"It's all very complicated, isn't it? Hard to keep track, I mean."
"Mh."
"So maybe Addie also got confused, and that's why she ran away?"
We had joined our usual lineup at cat choir, but while the other cats, and Dex Dexter in particular, were singing their hearts out, my own heart wasn't really in it, and I was merely going through the motions.
"Dooley, stop blabbing!" Shanille shouted. "And you, Max, start showing you care! And where the hell is Harriet—my star soprano!"
"She's chasing slugs and snails with Brutus!" said Dooley.
But Shanille, who hates interruptions, shushed him into

silence, and bellowed, "From the top! And this time, try to pretend you care, you two!"

And so the rehearsals went on.

It took me a while to work it out, but I think I finally managed halfway through a haunting rendition of an Adele song. It was around the same time that a shoe hit me in the rear and I toppled from my perch on top of the slide. Luckily I landed on all fours, and I don't know if it was the shoe or the soothing effect of the song, but a lightbulb seemed to go off in my head, and the word 'Eureka' was trembling on my lips as I finally saw the light. Or at least part of it.

I'd landed right in front of a snail, as it happened. Possibly one of the specimens that had infested our backyard earlier. It gave me its typical supercilious look that a lot of these snails seem to share, and turned away from me while making a sort of scoffing noise, before slithering back into the undergrowth whence it came.

Frédérique, who'd let rip an anguished cry as I was struck by said shoe, was gratified to see I was all right, and gave me a beaming smile. I'd already talked to her, and she'd told me that her human had displayed no suspicious behavior at all, unfortunately, but that she was hoping he still might at some point.

That evening, as soon as we arrived home, I told Odelia about my bright idea, and I could tell that it resonated with her as well, unlikely as it might sound.

And since I was going well, I decided to tell her about Gran and Marge and Tex's visit to Andrew Dexter, which caused her no small degree of surprise.

"They did what?!" she cried.

Chase, who'd been checking something on his phone, looked up at her outburst.

"The snails again?" he asked. He glanced over in the direction of the backyard. "They're back, aren't they?"

"It's not the snails," said Odelia, looking a little irate, I have to say. "It's my family. They've collectively lost their mind."

"It had to happen sometime, babe," said Chase consolingly. "They're old, you know, and old people sometimes get all doddery and weird."

"They're not that old," said Odelia. She gritted her teeth. "Wait till they get back."

"Okay, you got me. What happened?" asked Chase, his curiosity piqued.

"Gran saw me hug Edward Dexter—though now it looks like it wasn't Edward but his twin brother Andrew—and now she thinks I'm having an affair with the guy. And to make sure he breaks it off, she went over to his house to look for something she can hold over him."

Much to his credit, Chase actually laughed. But when Odelia shot him a furious look, he quickly stopped.

"It's funny!" he argued. "And besides, it shows how much they care."

"It shows how nuts they are," Odelia grumbled.

"Nuts, but in a good way."

"I just hope Andrew doesn't catch them in the act and files a complaint."

"Yeah, that wouldn't be good," said Chase, sobering. "They won't get caught. Your gran is getting pretty good at this kind of stuff."

"Laugh all you want, but it's not funny."

"It's a little funny, you have to admit."

But she shook her head stubbornly, having folded her arms across her chest. "So not funny," she insisted.

"Okay, so what's all this about Edward Dexter not being Edward Dexter?" said Chase, wisely changing the subject.

Odelia perked up. "Well, turns out Edward is actually his twin brother Andrew, and Addie isn't his daughter but his niece, and according to Andrew's cat Dex, who is actually Edward's cat, Addie isn't missing but is still on her road trip."

"Could be that Andrew didn't tell his cat what's going on."

"Yeah, that's possible. Not all people talk to their cats, I guess."

"No, they sure don't," said Chase with a grin.

"Oh, and Max has a theory."

"Of course he has."

"If I tell you, will you at least try to back me up when I tell off my family?"

"You know I will, babe."

"Don't act as if it's one big joke. This is serious."

"Absolutely. I'll back you up one hundred percent. They've gone too far this time."

"Which is exactly what I intend to tell them," she said.

It took a while for the trio to return home, having first dropped off Scarlett.

But when they came in, they looked as unhappy as any three unsuccessful conspirators could look. Looks like Gran hadn't managed to crack that safe after all.

"So what's all this I hear about you breaking into Mr. Dexter's place?" asked Odelia.

Marge and Tex seemed taken aback, but Gran immediately went on the counter-attack. "And what's all this about you and Dexter having an affair? And don't try to deny it, missy," she added, shaking a bony finger in her granddaughter's face. "Cause I saw it with my own two eyes! And I have proof!"

"All I did was give the guy a hug, cause he just told me his daughter went missing, and he was obviously feeling bad. There is no affair, there never was an affair, and you should know better than to think such things about me, Gran!"

Now it was Gran's turn to look startled. "You mean... you and Dexter..."

"There is no me and Dexter! I love my husband, and no Dexter will ever come between us!"

"Well spoken," Chase murmured.

"I knew I should have talked to you about it," said Marge.

"The pictures looked so convincing, though," said Tex.

"What pictures?" asked Odelia. And when her mom showed her the infamous pictures on her phone, she said, "You thought this was me having an affair? You're all nuts!"

"From a certain angle it looks as if you're kissing the guy," said Gran stubbornly.

"No, it doesn't. And besides, Max and Dooley were there. Didn't they tell you nothing was going on?"

"Yeah, they did," Gran confessed sheepishly. "I just figured they hadn't been looking. Either that or they were trying to protect you."

"God, what a mess," said Odelia, throwing up her arms.

"Is it true that you broke into Dexter's place?" asked Chase, a glint of amusement in his eye, which he tried hard to hide by employing his gruffest voice.

"Yeah, we did," said Gran. "Me and Scarlett broke in while Marge and Tex were distracting the guy. But we didn't find anything. Except he's got underwear with bitcoins printed on it. Which is just weird for a grown man, wouldn't you say?"

"It's hardly a crime," said Marge.

She was eying her daughter with a touch of anxiousness. "I'm sorry, honey," she said now. "I really thought something was going on between you and this billionaire. And the thought just made me sick."

"Yeah, we all love Chase, and we think he's the best thing that ever happened to you—and this family," Tex added.

"Gee, Tex," said Chase, "that's the nicest thing anyone has ever said to me."

"Well, it's true," said Tex fervently. "We love you, buddy."

"Yeah, we really do," said Marge.

Chase looked touched, and even Odelia's expression lost that edge.

"That's still no reason to harass perfectly innocent people," she said, but I could tell that her anger had expended itself, and she was ready to forgive and forget.

"I'm sorry," said Gran ruefully. "I overreacted. But I did it with the best intentions."

"I know you did, Gran," said Odelia, and for the next five minutes there was a lot of hugging and kissing and, in the case of Tex and Chase, backslapping.

In other words: time to get out of there!

And so Dooley and I quickly fled through the pet flap and into the backyard. When humans start getting sentimental, cats flee. It's one of those facts of life.

And that's when I caught a whiff of the same smell I'd experienced in Andrew Dexter's backyard. And I knew I'd solved my second mystery of the night. And when I caught sight of a particular bottle, there was no doubt in my mind I knew what had attracted this army of snails into our lovely backyards.

CHAPTER 37

Once again we'd entered the woods, for what I sincerely hoped would be the last time in quite a while. Some cats may love the woods—like our friend Clarice—and manage to survive out there, and even thrive, but I'm not such a cat. Give me my comfy couch and my bowl of kibble and my humans any time. Okay, so call me spoiled, but that's how I roll.

We'd arrived at the same clearing where not-Cyril Wellbeloved had almost put us in his pot the day before, but this time we'd come with a small but impressive contingent of humans, and so there would be no capturing us now.

Odelia was there, of course, and Chase, but also Uncle Alec, who wanted to find out firsthand what was going on out there.

Chase knocked on the door, and when no answer came, bellowed, "Police—open up!"

The door was reluctantly opened to a crack, and when not-Cyril caught sight of the four cats seated at our humans' feet, he said plaintively, "I wasn't really going to eat them.

And besides, how was I supposed to know they belonged to someone?"

"We're not here about the cats," Chase announced, producing his badge, as did Uncle Alec, and even Odelia. The only ones who didn't have a badge to show were yours truly and friends. But then cats don't have pockets, so that hampers our badge-carrying capacity to some extent.

"What's your name, sir?" asked Chase now.

"What's it to you?" the guy riposted.

"We can either do this down at the station or right now. What's your name?"

The guy gave Chase a look of defiance, but finally muttered something under his breath.

"I'm sorry, I didn't catch that," said Chase.

"Dexter," the guy repeated quietly. "Edward Dexter."

Odelia glanced down at me, and I gave her a knowing look.

"Well, Mr. Dexter, we have strong reasons to suspect that you've kidnapped your daughter Addie Dexter, and her boyfriend Ted Machosko, and are keeping them on the premises."

"I don't know what you're talking about," said Dexter. "My daughter lives with my brother Andrew, as everyone knows."

"No, she does not. She left home a couple of weeks ago to go on a road trip, only she never arrived."

"I don't know anything about that. You have to talk to my brother."

"We have talked to your brother. And he asked us to find his niece, since he's very worried about her safety and that of her boyfriend."

"I'm sorry, but I can't help you," said Dexter, clearly losing his patience. And as he made to close the door, Chase put his foot down—in the crack.

"We can do this the easy way, or the hard way," he said. "Either you tell us where she is, or we're going to search this place top to bottom until we find her. What's it going to be, Dexter?"

The guy hesitated, but when he saw the determined look of steel on the cop's face, and the equally steely look on Uncle Alec's, he finally relented. "Okay, fine. But don't blame me, all right? This was her idea from the start."

And as he threw the door wide, two more people looked out at us from inside the small shack. They were Addie Dexter and what I assumed was her boyfriend Ted.

"He's right," said Addie. "This isn't my dad's fault. It's mine."

"Addie Dexter?" asked Chase.

The girl nodded.

She looked a little primitive, with simple clothes, no makeup, and her hair cut short and unwashed. But otherwise unharmed.

"And you, sir? Who are you?" asked Chase.

"Ted Machosko," said the guy, a gangly kid with dark hair.

"And you both confirm that you're living here of your own free will?"

"That's right," said Addie. "We actually live down there," she added, gesturing to a spot at the edge of the clearing.

We all looked, but saw nothing.

"We live underground," Ted explained. "We buried the RV and turned it into an underground home. Cozy and cheap."

"Warm in the winter and cool in the summer," Addie added. "The perfect place, really. And very private, as you can see."

I saw nothing, but if they said the RV was there, I took their word for it.

"You do realize that your uncle is very worried about you?" said Odelia, with a touch of reproach in her voice.

"I know," said the girl, hanging her head. "And I was planning to tell him, but I knew he wouldn't approve, and would make me come back and live with him."

"But why? Why live out here?" asked Odelia.

"It's a long story," said the girl, interlocking fingers with her boyfriend. "Are you sure you want to hear it?"

"Absolutely," said Chase.

I think we all wanted to hear the story, not least of all Odelia, who'd spent so much time looking for this young woman.

"Okay, but not here," said Addie. "Let's go to the RV. It's a lot cozier down there—no offense, Dad."

"None taken," the man mumbled.

Now that I saw him again, I could see the resemblance with his brother, which is why he'd looked so familiar the first time. The beard masked a lot of his features, and also the fact that he hadn't really taken good care of himself. But there was no mistake: this was the real Edward Dexter. The billionaire.

"Why is a billionaire living in a shack in the woods, Max?" asked Dooley as we followed Addie and Ted in the direction of their cozy little home—underground.

"I think we're about to find out, Dooley," I said.

"He's probably one of those survivalists," said Brutus. "You know: a prepper."

"He doesn't look prepared to me," said Harriet. "More lost than ready."

We'd arrived at the edge of the clearing, and Ted reached down and pulled at something hidden under a clump of grass. It proved to be a hatch, and moments later we were all climbing down a ladder into a very roomy and spacious RV. It was like a small apartment, but underground. And as the lights switched on, it turned out to be a lot bigger than I thought. Clearly Andrew Dexter hadn't stinted when he bought his niece this RV. It must have been a top-of-the-line model.

"You've got electricity down here?" asked Chase, impressed.

"Yeah, Ed runs his own generator," Ted explained.

Addie led us into the living area, and the humans all took a seat around the table while Ted disappeared into the kitchen to rustle us up some coffee.

"Nice place you got here," said Uncle Alec, to break the ice. "Very, um... special."

"We like it," said Addie, who was a cheerful girl, and looked pretty happy and healthy to me.

"So why live out here?" asked Chase. "When you could live in luxury with your uncle?"

"Okay, so the thing is," said Addie, launching into her story, "that I've always known that one day I'd go look for my dad. Uncle Andrew said he didn't know where he was, but I had a feeling he was lying. Or that he must have some idea where he'd gone off to but wouldn't tell me. It took me until my final year in college to come up with a plan, and the support of Ted to set it up."

"So this whole road trip idea—that was just to find your dad?" asked Odelia.

"Yeah, pretty much. I knew my uncle wouldn't approve if I told him about my quest, so I came up with the road trip. Though we did have a lot of fun traveling from coast to coast. But my main destination was always Hampton Cove."

"How did you find out where your dad was?" asked Odelia, who gratefully accepted a cup of steaming hot coffee from Ted.

"That's Ted again," said Addie.

"I'm originally from around these parts," said Ted, also taking a seat. "Only my family moved west a couple of years ago. But so back when I was a kid, I was hiking out here with a buddy from school when we discovered this old shack. When we glanced in through the window, suddenly there was this horrible face staring back at us. We immediately took off, scared out of our wits. And that always stuck with me. Especially because just before the guy's face appeared, I'd seen a picture of the most beautiful girl in the world, pinned up on his wall."

Addie smiled, and took the young man's hand in hers.

"So many years later, when I met Addie in college, I thought there was something familiar about her. It took me a while to remember the picture, which is when I told her about the incident."

"Which is why I had to come and see," said Addie. "To find out if he was my dad. And he was."

"Edward had made his billions, but had a nervous breakdown of some kind," Ted explained. "He was in a real slump, and felt he needed to get away. To turn his back on his life and try to find himself again. So he ended up out here in the woods, and as months turned into years, he decided that he felt much better out here alone than back in the rat race of the corporate world he left behind."

"So he left his daughter in his brother's care?" asked Uncle Alec, who'd taken a very large chocolate chip cookie and was munching on it with visible relish.

"Not just his daughter. He left everything behind," said Ted. "His house, his business, his investments—his whole life."

"So you took your trip, and then you disappeared. Why?" asked Chase.

"Like I said, I knew my uncle wouldn't approve," said Addie. "I wanted to get to know my dad. Finding him again after all these years, it really means something to me. So I decided to stick around for a while. It was actually his idea to bury the RV, so we could live here. And Ted's been going into town to get supplies, making sure he's not recognized."

"You'd be surprised what a wig and a fake beard can do," said Ted with a grin.

"I wasn't going to go off the grid for too long," said Addie. "I don't want my uncle to worry, or to suffer, but I did think I deserved this time with my dad."

"This wasn't a long-term plan," said Ted. "Just a couple of weeks, tops."

"Though I should have known my uncle would try and find us," said Addie.

"He tried to be discreet about it," said Odelia. "He didn't want to attract too much attention to your disappearance."

"He must have been worried, though. Oh, I feel so bad about this now."

"There was no way he would have allowed you to live with your dad, sweetie," said Ted.

"I know, but still. He's been like a father to me all these years." She gave us a weak smile. "I'll go home soon, I promise. But these two weeks with my dad have been so important to me. And I really feel like we've established a genuine connection, you know. I mean, I can tell he's not okay. I'm not a psychologist, but I figure my mother's passing must have scarred him for life, and the stresses and pressures of his business didn't help, and so when he finally had a breakdown, it was a major one, and he still hasn't recovered. But I can also see that my presence has done him good. He seems better now than when we first arrived."

"He really does, doesn't he?" said Ted.

"Oh, absolutely. I think he might even be ready to meet his brother again."

"I have to say I'm impressed," said Uncle Alec, looking around at the RV's interior. "How much do you think a setup like this would set me back?"

"You're not thinking about buying an RV, are you, buddy?" asked Chase.

"Well, maybe not right now, but at some point, why not?" He smiled. "Charlene—that's my girlfriend—has been trying to persuade me to go on holiday together. First time as a couple. And I've been holding off. But traveling in an RV like this? I can definitely see that happening. Better than to lie on a beach someplace."

"You'd have to ask my uncle about the price," said Addie. "But knowing him, he probably got the best RV money can buy."

"I'll bet he won't be happy that they buried his nice RV," said Dooley.

"They could have just parked nearby," said Brutus. "Now they'll have to dig it up again, and clean it."

"I think they planned to stay here for much longer than Addie is letting on," I ventured. "Months, maybe. Only now that we found her, she'll have to change her plans."

"Oh, well. It was nice while it lasted," said Harriet, who was bored already. And I could totally see why: no pets, and so: no kibble!

Then again, what pet would live underground like this? Moles might like it, but not cats.

"Humans are strange, aren't they, Max?" said Dooley. "To live like this, just to be near their dad."

"It's a growing trend," I said. "Tiny houses and back to nature and all that. Perhaps more people will come and live out here, and follow Edward's example. Life for humans does get pretty stressful sometimes."

"I'd never be able to live out here," Brutus confessed. "I hate confined spaces."

And so we said our goodbyes to Addie and Ted, who promised they'd get in touch with her uncle soon.

"I really thought Addie was buried in our backyard," said

Brutus as we resurfaced and breathed in that wonderful forest air once more.

"Why?" asked Harriet.

"Well, the snails," he said. "They are attracted to dead and rotting stuff, and so I thought Addie must be out there."

"It wasn't dead and rotting stuff the snails were attracted to," I said.

"Oh?" said Brutus. "Then what?"

I smiled. "Blue moon!"

CHAPTER 38

The sun was giving of its best and so was Tex. Even his backyard was getting back on its feet, and here and there fresh green was already poking its head, indicating that pretty soon everything would be as verdant and colorful as before.

Tex had been manning the grill, and supplying us all with sustenance, and for the occasion actual chicken was on the menu, and it tasted like chicken, too!

"What's that bottle of beer doing on the table, Max?" asked Dooley.

"It's the beer I told you about," I said. "Don't you remember? Blue Moon beer?"

"Oh, that's right. The beer that snails like so much."

"They don't like it, they love it," I said. "Snails can smell beer from up to two hundred yards away."

"I never knew snails liked beer," said Harriet. "It makes me like them even less, to be honest."

"It's not the beer itself they like, but the yeast it contains. Snails love yeast."

"You shouldn't have done it is all I'm saying," said Alec for the umpteenth time.

"And I keep telling you I did it because I thought it was the right thing to do," said Gran. "Tex was complaining that his begonias were wilting, and Marge kept saying how terrible her forsythias looked this year, and so I decided to give them a helping hand."

"By pouring beer on them," said Alec, shaking his head.

"It sounded like a good idea!"

"Where have I heard that before?" said Scarlett with a slight grin, earning herself a light slap on the arm from her friend.

"Dick Bernstein said it made his plants grow twice as fast. He swears by Blue Moon beer. Says it's the best fertilizer known to man. And who am I to question the guy? You should see his bush. It's luxuriant, big... Everything a bush should be."

"Please stop talking about Dick's bush," said Marge with a look of distaste. "I'm eating."

"I think he was pulling your leg," said Odelia. "Like that time he told Dad that mayonnaise can cure hair loss and he smeared the stuff all over his head. Remember?"

Smiling faces told us that everyone remembered, and Tex, whose hair loss had improved, said, "I think it worked."

"It wasn't the mayonnaise that did the trick, honey," said Marge. "But that special shampoo Scarlett got you."

"Chinese medicine," said Scarlett. "You can't go wrong with Chinese medicine."

"I don't like Chinese medicine," said Uncle Alec. "Charlene once sent me to an acupuncturist. He stuck me full of needles."

"That's what an acupuncturist does, sweetie," said Charlene.

"Well, I didn't like it. It hurt."

"Oh, poor baby," said Charlene with a grin at Marge. "So when are we going to start looking at RVs?"

"Next week."

"You said that last week."

"So what happened with the snails?" asked Dooley. "I still don't get it."

"Gran asked Dick Bernstein how he managed to grow his bushes so luxuriant," I explained, "and Dick told her that he sprayed Blue Moon beer on them. So Gran doused the entire backyard with beer, attracting so many snails they destroyed everything that grew."

"Which may or may not have been Dick's plan," said Harriet. "Since there's a garden competition coming up, and Gran had told Dick she was thinking of entering our backyard for the competition."

"So he sabotaged her. Bad man," said Brutus as he tucked into a piece of chicken.

"What I don't understand," said Marge, "is how Odelia's backyard, and also Ted and Marcie's, attracted all of those snails."

Gran gave her a sheepish look. "I may have repeated the same procedure on Odelia's backyard, and on Ted and Marcie's, when they weren't looking." When howls of disapproval met her words, she cried, "I just wanted to help!"

"Well, next time, don't," Uncle Alec grunted.

"At least the snails are gone now," said Harriet. "I hate those slithery, slimy creatures."

"They say it's very good for the skin, though," said Brutus. "And the fur."

This had Harriet looking up with interest. "You don't say."

"Yes, it's true. It's got antioxidant properties, stimulates collagen production and enhances wound healing. I saw it on the internet. And we all know that everything you see on the internet is true."

Oh, boy.

"So is Addie home again?" asked Marge.

"Yeah, she is," said Odelia.

"I think what you did is such a good thing," said Charlene. "And Alec tells me she's reunited with her dad?"

"Yeah, he won't leave the woods," said Odelia, "but she visits him as often as she can, and her regular visits are having a very positive effect on him. Last time we talked she told me he's even started using the shower they had installed, and has been wearing the fresh clothes she brings him every week. She does his laundry," she explained for her grandmother's sake.

"A girl shouldn't do her dad's laundry," the old lady grumbled. "That's just wrong."

"Well, she does it with a lot of love, and clearly the treatment is working, for he even met his brother for the first time in years, and the reunion was touching."

"I'm glad that all is well that ends well," said Marge. "And to think that I thought you and Mr. Dexter were having an affair." She directed a scathing look at her mother, who threw up her arms.

"They were hugging!" Gran cried.

"I hug Dolores all the time," said Uncle Alec as he popped a French fry into his mouth, "and you don't see me having an affair with her."

Charlene blinked. "You hug Dolores?"

"Well... yeah," he said, flinching a little.

"You never told me."

"Well, I wouldn't, would I? It's just one of those things."

"One of what things?"

"It's a tough job to be a dispatcher, and so sometimes... She's feeling bad... and so she needs a hug... and, well, I give it to her."

"Uh-oh," said Harriet. "Looks like Uncle Alec made a boo-boo."

"Boo-boo!" Grace cried, who was sitting on the swing right next to us.

"Do you think Uncle Alec and Dolores are having an affair?" asked Dooley.

"No, Dooley, they're not," I said.

Though from the look on Gran's face, I had the distinct impression that she thought he was. No smoke without fire!

Just then, a tiny voice sounded in my rear, and when I turned, I saw that once again we were in the presence of Rupert.

"Oh, hey, Rupert," I said. "I haven't thanked you for that tip about Blue Moon beer."

"I knew you'd get it," said Rupert as he crawled along the wall until he'd reached eye level. "And there's something else I wanted to tell you, but it seems to have escaped me for the present." He shrugged. "It'll come to me, I'm sure."

"Oh, Rupert!" Harriet cried. "Is it true that the slime you produce is beneficial for the skin and fur?"

"Oh, sure," said Rupert. "Best natural skin cream in the world."

"You don't say."

"But I do. Have you ever seen a snail with wrinkles?"

"So could you... walk on my face, maybe?"

Rupert made a face. "Um..."

Just then, a loud cry of anguish rang out. It seemed to come from next door. Next thing we knew, Marcie's head popped up over the hedge. "My rose bushes—they're full of snails! They're destroying everything!"

"Oh, now I remember," said Rupert. "I heard some of my friends call for a party next door. Something about beer for everyone."

Marge eyed her mother with a penetrating look. "Ma. What did you do?"

Gran gave a sort of feeble smile. "Well, I had to dump the rest of that beer somewhere, didn't I?"

THE END

Thanks for reading! If you want to know when a new Nic Saint book comes out, sign up for Nic's mailing list: nicsaint.com/news

EXCERPT FROM PURRFECT MATCH (MAX 54)

Chapter One

The atmosphere in the offices of the Advantage Publishing Company was as electric as ever. The publisher of such well-known publications as *Glimmer*, *Glitter* and *Vigor*—the magazine for the virile man—was considered by friend and foe as a regular powerhouse of the publishing industry. But with the diminished returns publishers saw on their print portfolio these days, and the ongoing transition to digital, tensions were running high in the hallowed halls of publishing. And nowhere was this more apparent than at the desk of Natalie Ferrara, located next to the corner office occupied by Advantage bigwig and CEO Michael Madison.

Natalie had been Mike Madison's personal assistant for going on five years, and in that time had fallen for her handsome boss's charms in a major way. So much so that she now found herself in trouble. Big trouble.

She was an attractive young woman of twenty-seven, with shiny hair the color of honey, cornflower-blue eyes and the kind of face and figure that could launch a thousand

EXCERPT FROM PURRFECT MATCH (MAX 54)

ships. What it hadn't managed, though, was to induce Michael Madison to divorce Mrs. Madison and make an honest woman out of his mistress.

Natalie pressed a tissue to her eyes. She was feeling particularly leaky again, and much to her embarrassment could not stop crying. If Mike saw her like this…

Oh, who was she kidding? Her boss's affections for her had taken a major dive in recent weeks. In fact she could pinpoint the exact date Natalie Ferrara stock had crashed and burned: when she had announced that she was pregnant, and that in due course a baby was going to be born who, if it was a boy, would no doubt inherit his daddy's firm jawline and no-nonsense attitude to life and business, and if it was a girl, hopefully would look more like her mother.

Contrary to what Natalie had expected, or secretly hoped, Michael had reacted to the news in the worst possible way, and had told her what he thought of the future prospects of his offspring by giving her the name of an excellent abortion clinic, offering to pay for the termination. He'd even said she could have the week off, and had grinned and clearly expected her to show her gratefulness by yipping with joy and throwing her arms around his neck and showering him with kisses.

Instead, she'd spent the entire weekend crying her eyes out, and now, two weeks later, she was still crying.

The fact that her brother Luke chose this exact moment to show up on her doorstep and foist his obnoxious personality on her, only added to her distress.

Loud noises emanating from Michael's office tore her away from her musings on the terrible fate that had befallen her, and for a moment her hand hovered over the phone, ready to call security.

Howard White, the well-known designer and *enfant*

EXCERPT FROM PURRFECT MATCH (MAX 54)

terrible of the fashion world, had had his run-ins with Michael before, but today sounded worse than usual.

"How dare you!" the eccentric fashion icon screamed. "You, sir, are a louse, a nitwit, a parasite, sucking the blood of the real talent: me! And you dare to criticize me? Me?!"

Natalie's hand relaxed. She really couldn't imagine Howard actually getting physical with Michael, who was a full head taller than he was, twenty-five years younger, and had about thirty pounds on the man, all hard-packed muscle, as she knew from personal experience.

Suddenly the door to the CEO's office swung open and a furious Howard stormed out. He was dressed in one of his own creations: a colorful kaftan hemmed with gold thread. His assistant Sebastian Lipskey was also with him. Neither of the men offered her a single glance as they passed her desk. Then they were gone. And good riddance, too, as far as Natalie was concerned.

Michael appeared at the door, his smoothly shaven face working as he watched the departure of the fashion mogul. He gave Natalie a pointed look, and grunted, "My office, Miss Ferrara. Now!"

And once again Natalie found herself scurrying into the CEO's office. Only this time probably not for a quick session of hot nookie.

Tom Mitchell, who sat two desks behind Natalie, watched the secretary's hurried entry into Madison's inner realm. Unlike the CEO, he had noticed Natalie's red eyes and her tears, no matter how hard she tried to hide them under a thick layer of makeup. Clearly the girl was in trouble, and even though the source of her trouble was unknown to Tom, Natalie's visible distress weighed heavily on him.

EXCERPT FROM PURRFECT MATCH (MAX 54)

For Tom had some trouble of his own to deal with, namely his unrequited affections for the golden-haired secretary, which had been plaguing him from the moment he'd started work at Advantage three years ago. All this time he'd been admiring the lovely young woman from afar, knowing she would never be his.

It had been made clear to him from day one to whom Natalie's affections in fact belonged: her affair with the big boss wasn't exactly a big secret. And many was the time he'd seen her sneak into his office, the blinds being pulled, the door being locked, and certain sounds emanating from the office that were more appropriate in a nature documentary than in the offices of a prominent CEO.

Then again, Michael Madison, as far as Tom had been able to ascertain, ticked all the boxes of your classic industry chieftain: he was brash, overconfident, narcissistic, uber-ambitious, and had a wandering eye and ditto hands.

But even though this affair had pretty much sunk Natalie's stock amongst her fellow staffers, it hadn't put a dent in Tom's secret affections. That young man's heart had belonged to Natalie from the moment he first laid eyes on her, and as far as he was concerned, would always remain that way, now and forever.

But since no one likes to wait for now or even forever, he decided to put pen to paper—or rather fingers to keyboard—and pour his heart out in a message to Hampton Cove's favorite agony column. And so he began: 'Dear Gabi...'

Three rows behind Tom, Doris Booth sat silently fuming as she stared at the gift Michael had left on her desk that morning. It was a copy of Strunk & White's *Elements of Style*. The

EXCERPT FROM PURRFECT MATCH (MAX 54)

perfect gift for anyone struggling with the basic tenets of grammar and spelling.

As the main publicist for *Glimmer*, language was Doris's forte. It was her secret weapon and her proudest possession both. And now here this horrible man had basically told her she couldn't spell?

In the immortal words of Howard White: how dare he! And as her mouth closed with the clicking sound of her perfect white teeth, in one smooth movement she dumped the precious little tome into her wastepaper basket, and picked up her phone to call the HR department.

If Michael Madison wanted a fight, he got one!

Chapter Two

One of the perks of being a cat is that you get to spend so much time with members of the human species. We all know that humans are weird, but they're also weirdly entertaining. In fact I can spend hours watching humans being, well, human. And it was exactly such an opportunity we were having now, watching Tex Poole, our human's dad, engaged in an activity he called 'clearing the attic.'

You have to understand that part of the human experience is to collect junk. Piles and piles of junk. And then at some point, usually in the spring, they suddenly get tired of this pile of junk and start moving it from one place to another. In this case Tex was moving the pile from his attic to the sidewalk, where he hoped other humans would take it away and add it to their own little pile.

It's one of those human pastimes that's simply fascinating for a people watcher like myself, and so I was having a great time watching this particular human now.

"Why is Tex putting all this junk on the sidewalk, Max?"

EXCERPT FROM PURRFECT MATCH (MAX 54)

asked Dooley, who marveled at the sheer volume of stuff the Pooles had amassed in such a small space.

"He hopes other humans will take it away," I said.

"But why did he collect it in the first place?"

"Now that," I said, "is a mystery I still haven't figured out."

I may be an amateur detective, but there are mysteries that are simply too deep to fathom.

Tex had donned an old pair of jeans, an old sweater, and had put a baseball cap on top of his head, as he rooted through the stuff collected in his attic, and it really was a sight to behold, as he opened a box, and either uttered cries of ecstasy, or agony. Ecstasy when he found an old train set he'd played with as a boy, agony when he came upon one of Gran's treasures. Such as there are: 'priceless' artifacts she'd picked up at some garage sale in the year of our Lord 1977. Or the oddly shaped—or oddly misshaped, depending on the eye of the beholder—clay pots that were the product of a pottery class she took in the early eighties.

"Will you look at that?" Tex muttered when he opened yet another old box and took out a tattered little booklet. "I used to read these all the time!"

A glance told me it was a booklet in a series featuring the Hardy Boys.

"Who are the Hardy Boys, Max?" asked Dooley, not missing a beat. "Are they boys that are very hardy?"

"I suppose so," I said. Of course they'd have to be hardy to survive up there in the attic for all these years. At least the attic was dry, but it was also dusty, and not a lot of fun to hang around in for long periods of time.

And so when Tex settled down to read his copy of these hardy Hardy Boys, we decided to take a break from watching him, and go and do the other thing that we enjoy so much: take long naps on any surface we find agreeable. Today I decided to check out the new comforter Chase had brought home with him, and had been extolling the virtues of when he and Odelia put it on the bed that morning.

And as we settled down, I remembered how Chase had said, a catch in his voice, that this would be the first time he and his lady love would get to have first dibs at this nice new thing they got.

How cute humans are. And how naive.

While Tex was thus engrossed in the adventures of Frank and Joe Hardy, as chronicled by Franklin W. Dixon, keen eyes had spotted the growing pile of attic surplus on the sidewalk. It just so happened that a troop of girl scouts had selected this particular day to traipse up and down the neighborhood to spread some sweetness and light in the form of girl scout cookies, and so when they turned up on the doorstep of 46 Harrington Street, hoping to extract some coin from the Poole family, their attention was momentarily distracted by the remnants of Tex and Marge Poole's past. So much so that one of their lot, a smallish freckled specimen answering to the name Mabel, felt compelled to pick up a shoebox and take a look inside.

It is, after all, not just cats that marvel at the strange things humans do. Little boys and girls—hardy or not hardy—are just the same. And when Mabel found a stack of letters inside this box, neatly tied together with a red ribbon and a bow, she gibbered excitedly, "You guys, look what I found!"

The other girls of her troop all trooped around, putting their cookie-dispensing mission on hold for the nonce, and gibbered just as excitedly as Mabel extricated the bundle of letters from its receptacle, and gently relieved it from its red ribbon.

"The mailman must have dropped them," said Mabel,

EXCERPT FROM PURRFECT MATCH (MAX 54)

holding the letters reverently. Her daddy was a mailman, and she loved her daddy very much, and had a fervent reverence for the mysterious profession he was engaged in. Handing out presents in the form of letters every day just seemed like such a nice thing to do!

"We have to help the mailman," said a precocious girl with braces named Jackie.

"Jackie is right," a third girl named Frida announced earnestly. "If we don't help the mailman the people these letters are for are going to be very unhappy. My daddy didn't get a letter once and he was so upset he wrote a letter to the post office."

"Your daddy wrote a letter to get a letter?" asked a fourth girl.

Frida nodded, a serious expression on her face. "It was an important letter."

"But how did he know the letter hadn't arrived if it hadn't arrived?" asked a fifth girl, evidencing a keen logic.

This had Jackie stumped for a while, but she quickly rallied. "He must have had a letter telling him he'd get the letter, which is how he knew he didn't get the letter. The second letter, I mean, not the first, which is when he wrote the third letter."

Nods of understanding made the girls' heads bob up and down like a stadium wave, but then Mabel drew their attention to the problem at hand once more.

She was still holding the letters in her grubby little hands. "So what now?" she asked. She'd discovered that the letters were closed, the flaps tucked neatly into their designated opposite flaps, and that there were nice stamps on the letters, and an address written in a sort of spidery scrawl. If she'd been a regular visitor to the doctor, she would have recognized the near-illegible handwriting as typical for your up-and-coming medico. But since her reading skills weren't all that well-developed yet, she had a hard time deciphering the address.

One of the other girls said they all seemed to be addressed to the same street: Harrington Street. And Mabel, whose daddy sometimes talked shop during dinner, said, "This means that all these letters are for people on this street."

"So let's post them," Jackie suggested. "And let's make all the people happy."

The idea warmed Mabel's heart. The notion of an undelivered letter gave this mailman's daughter the pip, and so the mission quickly took on the nature of a sacred assignment. A mission to help all mail-persons the world over.

The next few minutes were spent separating the stack of letters into equal piles, to be divided amongst the members of the troop. It took a while, for there were sixteen letters in all, but only five members, and sixteen doesn't divide by five, so one of the girls was going to have to distribute six letters instead of five. But since Mabel had made this great find, she took it upon herself to carry the extra load.

And it must be said, she did it with gusto. If one good deed promises an uplifted heart and a happy community, imagine what six good deeds will do!

And as Marge Poole idly gazed out of the window, nursing a cup of coffee, and wondering why five girl scouts were rummaging through the pile of attic detritus her husband had placed on the sidewalk, the love letters Tex had written to her more than twenty-five years ago, during a brief but intense courtship, were now on the verge of being redistributed amongst the couple's friends and neighbors.

Chapter Three

Popular opinion has it that cats don't enjoy the company

EXCERPT FROM PURRFECT MATCH (MAX 54)

of other cats. That we're solitary animals and won't tolerate the kind of intrusion to our peace and quiet other cats—or even dogs—bring. And I have to say that on the whole I don't mind living in a household with three other cats. But sometimes it gets too much. Like today, for instance. I'd just plunged into that pleasant state of drowsiness that is so rewarding, when a sharp voice hauled me out of my slumber.

"Max! What are you doing?"

It was Harriet, entering the bedroom, clearly on the lookout for yours truly.

"I was sleeping," I announced, lazily opening one eye to take in the newcomer.

"How do I look?" she asked, and since I know that Harriet won't take satisfaction from just a cursory glance, I opened my second eye to give her the once-over.

"You look... like you always look," I said, hedging my bets.

"In other words..." she insisted, not letting me off the hook.

"Great!" I said, injecting a modicum of cheerfulness into my voice, inasmuch as one can be cheerful to the person who's just interrupted a perfectly nice nap.

"You could be more specific, Max," she lamented. "Great is so generic."

"Well..." I said, going through my mental thesaurus. "You look, um, amazing?"

But her grimace told me I was wide off the mark. "You, Dooley?" she said.

Dooley, who's often slower than me in the waking-up department, blinked and stared at our friend, not comprehending. "Me Dooley," he said finally. "You Harriet?"

"Oh, for crying out loud!" Harriet said, rolling a pair of very expressive green eyes. "Can I get some constructive criticism here, *por favor*?"

Brutus, who'd also wandered into the room, now said,

EXCERPT FROM PURRFECT MATCH (MAX 54)

"You look radiant, sweet pea. Your fur is shinier than the brightest diamond, your eyes are like the twin pools of a crystal mountain lake, and your visage the epitome of loveliness."

Brutus had clearly been reading love poems again. Lately he's taken to browsing websites that cater to the amateur poet, and it showed.

"Oh, sweetie pie," said Harriet, her voice suddenly a purr. "Now *that's* the kind of stuff your budding model likes to hear. You don't think I'm too fat, do you?"

"Not too fat," said Brutus quickly. "Slim like a reed swaying in the breeze."

"Mh," said Harriet. Clearly this particular simile wasn't as apt as the others.

"What's all this about a budding model?" I asked. I might have been napping, but that didn't mean my brain had been fully switched off.

Harriet preened a little. "Guess who's been selected to feature on the cover of next month's *Cat Life*?"

"Fifi?" Dooley suggested, referring to our canine neighbor.

"*CAT Life*, Dooley," Harriet snapped. "Not *Dog Life*."

Dooley thought hard, then finally brightened. "Shanille?"

"No, not Shanille!" Harriet cried. "Me, Dooley, me!"

"You?" asked Dooley, and his surprise was so palpable it took the bloom off the rose of Harriet's excitement, for she directed a dark frown at my friend. Dooley, being Dooley, hardly noticed. "But why you?" he insisted. "You're not a model."

"Well, I'm a model now, so you better get used to it," she said. "And incidentally, you've all been recruited as members of my team."

"And what team is that?" asked Dooley innocently.

EXCERPT FROM PURRFECT MATCH (MAX 54)

"Team Harriet, what else?" she snapped, her patience wearing thin.

"I didn't know you played football," said Dooley, interested.

"Oh, Dooley," Harriet sighed, then turned to me. "I want you to be my spotter, Max."

"Your what?" I asked, stifling a yawn.

"Spotter. You're going to keep a close eye on me and tell me if anything is off."

I stared at her. I could see a lot that was off, but didn't know if it was a good idea to tell her. Her lack of respect for a person's nap time, for one thing.

Brutus, who could see I was struggling with the concept, now piped up, "A person changes from day to day, Max. And the weird thing is that you don't always notice such changes yourself. So it's up to others to draw your attention to them."

"And what changes would this be?" I asked carefully.

"The luster of my coat, for one thing," said Harriet, holding out a paw. "Or the absence of spots on my nose, for another."

"So Max has to spot your spots?" asked Dooley, trying valiantly to keep up.

"Yes, Dooley," said Harriet with an expressive eyeroll. "Max has to spot my spots."

"And me?" asked Dooley, who seemed to like this new game. "What do you want me to do?"

Harriet gave him a look of such disdain it would have frozen a lesser cat dead on the spot. But not Dooley, who was genuinely excited about the prospect of becoming something big on Team Harriet, whatever it was.

"You can watch my diet," she said after a moment's reflection. "Make sure I don't eat anything fattening, or generally designed to disagree with me."

EXCERPT FROM PURRFECT MATCH (MAX 54)

"So you want me to chew your food for you?" asked Dooley, puzzled.

"Eww, Dooley! I do not want you to chew my food for me! All I'm asking—and if it's too much to ask, just tell me—is that you keep an eye on my caloric intake."

"Your colic…"

"*Caloric.*"

"Um…"

"Just make sure she doesn't eat junk food," Brutus clarified.

Dooley gave me a look of surprise. If ever there was a cat who doesn't allow anyone to come between her and a nice bowl of junk food, it was Harriet. The more additives and colorants and artificial flavoring her wet food contains, the better she likes it. Then again, I guess all cats love the tasty stuff. I know I do. But that doesn't mean I'd attack the person denying it to me with tooth and claw.

"Okay," said Dooley finally, but I could tell that his excitement had waned.

"So Max," said Harriet, "first thing every morning, I want a status report."

"Gotcha," I said.

"And Dooley, you make sure I stick to a healthy and nutritious diet."

"Oh, all right," my friend murmured.

"And me?" asked Brutus. "What do you want me to do, honey blossom?"

Harriet offered her mate a bright smile. "You are my motivation coach, sugar plum. You make sure my energy levels are at an all-time high, all the time. Make sure I'm happy, happy, happy, and keep anything that might upset me away from me. Because we all know that what really matters isn't what's down here," she said, making a circular motion encompassing her face, but what's up here." She tapped her noggin. "It's all about the psychology, baby!"

"Yes, baby!" Brutus echoed, but judging from the look of anguish that I could read in his eyes, his own psychology was in need of a high-energy boost, too!

ABOUT NIC

Nic has a background in political science and before being struck by the writing bug worked odd jobs around the world (including but not limited to massage therapist in Mexico, gardener in Italy, restaurant manager in India, and Berlitz teacher in Belgium).

When he's not writing he enjoys curling up with a good (comic) book, watching British crime dramas, French comedies or Nancy Meyers movies, sampling pastry (apple cake!), pasta and chocolate (preferably the dark variety), twisting himself into a pretzel doing morning yoga, going for a run, and spoiling his big red tomcat Tommy.

He lives with his wife (and aforementioned cat) in a small village smack dab in the middle of absolutely nowhere and is probably writing his next 'Mysteries of Max' book right now.

www.nicsaint.com

ALSO BY NIC SAINT

The Mysteries of Max
Purrfect Murder
Purrfectly Deadly
Purrfect Revenge
Purrfect Heat
Purrfect Crime
Purrfect Rivalry
Purrfect Peril
Purrfect Secret
Purrfect Alibi
Purrfect Obsession
Purrfect Betrayal
Purrfectly Clueless
Purrfectly Royal
Purrfect Cut
Purrfect Trap
Purrfectly Hidden
Purrfect Kill
Purrfect Boy Toy
Purrfectly Dogged
Purrfectly Dead
Purrfect Saint
Purrfect Advice
Purrfect Passion

A Purrfect Gnomeful

Purrfect Cover

Purrfect Patsy

Purrfect Son

Purrfect Fool

Purrfect Fitness

Purrfect Setup

Purrfect Sidekick

Purrfect Deceit

Purrfect Ruse

Purrfect Swing

Purrfect Cruise

Purrfect Harmony

Purrfect Sparkle

Purrfect Cure

Purrfect Cheat

Purrfect Catch

Purrfect Design

Purrfect Life

Purrfect Thief

Purrfect Crust

Purrfect Bachelor

Purrfect Double

Purrfect Date

Purrfect Hit

Purrfect Baby

Purrfect Mess

Purrfect Paris

Purrfect Model

Purrfect Slug

The Mysteries of Max Box Sets

Box Set 1 (Books 1-3)

Box Set 2 (Books 4-6)

Box Set 3 (Books 7-9)

Box Set 4 (Books 10-12)

Box Set 5 (Books 13-15)

Box Set 6 (Books 16-18)

Box Set 7 (Books 19-21)

Box Set 8 (Books 22-24)

Box Set 9 (Books 25-27)

Box Set 10 (Books 28-30)

Box Set 11 (Books 31-33)

Box Set 12 (Books 34-36)

Box Set 13 (Books 37-39)

Box Set 14 (Books 40-42)

Box Set 15 (Books 43-45)

Box Set 16 (Books 46-48)

Box Set 17 (Books 49-51)

The Mysteries of Max Big Box Sets

Big Box Set 1 (Books 1-10)

Big Box Set 2 (Books 11-20)

The Mysteries of Max Shorts

Purrfect Santa (3 shorts in one)

Purrfectly Flealess

Purrfect Wedding

Purrfect Fuzz

Purrfect Love

Nora Steel

Murder Retreat

The Kellys

Murder Motel

Death in Suburbia

Emily Stone

Murder at the Art Class

Washington & Jefferson

First Shot

Alice Whitehouse

Spooky Times

Spooky Trills

Spooky End

Spooky Spells

Ghosts of London

Between a Ghost and a Spooky Place

Public Ghost Number One

Ghost Save the Queen

Box Set 1 (Books 1-3)

A Tale of Two Harrys

Ghost of Girlband Past

Ghostlier Things

Charleneland

Deadly Ride

Final Ride

Neighborhood Witch Committee

Witchy Start

Witchy Worries

Witchy Wishes

Saffron Diffley

Crime and Retribution

Vice and Verdict

Felonies and Penalties (Saffron Diffley Short 1)

The B-Team

Once Upon a Spy

Tate-à-Tate

Enemy of the Tates

Ghosts vs. Spies

The Ghost Who Came in from the Cold

Witchy Fingers

Witchy Trouble

Witchy Hexations

Witchy Possessions

Witchy Riches

Box Set 1 (Books 1-4)

The Mysteries of Bell & Whitehouse

One Spoonful of Trouble

Two Scoops of Murder

Three Shots of Disaster

Box Set 1 (Books 1-3)

A Twist of Wraith

A Touch of Ghost

A Clash of Spooks

Box Set 2 (Books 4-6)

The Stuffing of Nightmares

A Breath of Dead Air

An Act of Hodd

Box Set 3 (Books 7-9)

A Game of Dons

Standalone Novels

When in Bruges

The Whiskered Spy

ThrillFix

Homejacking

The Eighth Billionaire

The Wrong Woman

Printed in Great Britain
by Amazon